" She became marble, and listlessly watched him pour some fluid into
a cup of water on the table.'   See page 108.

The King's Gallant

OR

King Henry III. and His Court

("HENRI III. ET SA COUR")

A NOVELIZATION OF THE FAMOUS DRAMA

BY

ALEXANDRE DUMAS

AUTHOR OF

"D'ARTAGNAN, THE KING MAKER," "THE COUNT OF MONTE CRISTO,"
"THE THREE MUSKETEERS," ETC.

Translated by HENRY L. WILLIAMS

Fredonia Books
Amsterdam, The Netherlands

The King's Gallant
Or King Henry III. and His Court

by
Alexandre Dumas

ISBN: 1-58963-707-0

Reprinted from the 1902 edition

Fredonia Books
Amsterdam, The Netherlands
http://www.fredoniabooks.com

CONTENTS.

CONTENTS

PREFACE.

"The King's Gallant" is deserving of recognition, in that it is not only a novelization of one of the earliest of Dumas' plays, but it marked a distinct triumph in his career.

When "Henri III. et sa Cour" first appeared, it was sneered at, then denounced; but the great French dramatist believed in his work, and, after a season of storm and stress, it put to flight the purblind critics, crushing their fossil pleas for continuance of the long-winded and very mechanical speeches and labored action that were part and parcel of plays of the period.

Instead of bewigged and thickly-powdered heroes, whose natural forms had never been seen by the profane, and whose movements were clogged by artificial trammels, these characters in the court of King Henry the Third became living beings in their vivid encompassments: the Louvre Palace, the tragical halls of Blois Castle, the magician's sinister study, the roaring wineshops, and the tortuous streets of Old Paris, crowded with "the Leaguers," and beset by the Huguenots.

Admittedly, the sybarite prince was a washed-out replica of his ancestors, like Francis the First, but he had interesting if not amiable traits: provoking wit, fine cunning, as well as sincere friendship for those who served him well. If called upon he could display courage not unworthy his Curled Darlings who could fight as well as dance.

This makes it so marked to oppose him to the warrior prince, "Henry of the Scarface," the terrifying Duke of Guise, as easy in his battered armor as they in their silken and feathered costumes, though he could not domineer over them as over his age, haughty with racial pride, indolent with excessive bravery, grim in humor, unscrupulous in carrying out wide and high-reaching aims. Fighting like Cæsar, he made love—like Nero!

This was a tug of the Fox and the Bear, and its result is not flattering to either; but then the Bear should not have made an enemy of the Lion!

What a stirring age Dumas selected for his canvas! Statesmen could not repose; Catherine de Medici, that Semiramis of Italy and France, mother of three kings in their turn, reigning all the time, in the background, shaping the course of kingdoms in Rome as in Savoy, in Madrid as in Brussels, and keeping poison bowl and dagger as busy as the bravo's sword.

Hence, "the gallants" were forced to form an impenetrable phalanx around their enervated king, like inextinguishable stars around a "dead" planet.

This gives the zest to the variety among them: Joyeuse, verifying his name with his flowing fun; Epernon the prudent, striving to

rise on others' ruin; Bussy the over-bold, and
St. Megrin, the heroic knight, who was made
perfect by his passion becoming his sole
motive.

His tender, steady flame for the lovable, persecuted princess, remote from her home and in
a tyrannical power; his head fruitful in expe-
dients, his hand as apt to attack as to defend,
his heart bounding to avenge and chastise. He
is an idol for those who have a cherished corner
for a shrine worthy of such Scipios.

If this work is full with the rushing sap of
spring's apple-trees, it is because Dumas was
but a youth when he wrote it; but a youth who,
later on, made the delighted French proclaim
him their "Wizard of Fiction."

Belonging to the Series of "The Lady of
Monsoreau," "Chicot the Jester," and "The
Forty-five," Dumas evinces his versatility by
never in a line repeating himself. Thus, "The
King's Gallant" is as the Benjamin of a family
full of favorites.   H. L. W.

THE KING'S GALLANT.

CHAPTER I.

THE ROYAL FAVORITES.

Of all the sluggard kings with whom France was burdened, none desired peace and quietness more than King Henry III. Yet not only was his reign disturbed by civil wars, but his capital city was kept in a turmoil by dissensions among his chief nobles, who bitterly hated one another, and made little effort to hide their feelings.

Among the most aspiring and least to be depended upon was the famous Henry "Scarface," the Duke of Guise, who headed the important movement against the reformers known as the "Holy League."

In forming this party, to dethrone the king if need be, and take his place, Guise had ample to engage him. But he was ensnared by Cupid, and trammeled his political plans by choosing as the object of his love a princess from over the Rhine.

This Princess of Potcian, daughter of the Duke of Cleves, was so unparalleled a beauty that her fame preceded her to Paris, where her godmother, Catherine de Medici, installed her. The gallants pressed around her until Scarface, her betrothed, compelled her to be put under a kind of restraint at Soissons House.

In addition, he established a service of espial upon her, beginning more to fear a loss of her than of the crown which he coveted.

As he sat in his study in Lorraine House, he presented much more of the warrior of that hard and cruel time than the court lover. Henry of Lorraine, Duke of Guise, surnamed "the Scarface (*Balafré*)," on account of a wound on his cheek, needed not this disfigurement to be soured with life at court, where good looks outweigh all moral traits.

Proud, haughty, ardent in sport and warfare, he donned with equal ease the still ponderous armor in vogue with knights inured to it from boyhood, or the most magnificent court attire. He could be agreeable enough, but as he felt his superiority to most of his political antagonists, he allowed his eyes to shoot out forbidding glances; he had in his campaigns so often cast dread that he delighted in suggesting what farther desolation lay in his power. The peers accounted him perfidious; those whom he had overthrown called him hard and cruel, and the lowly detested him.

His cold and pitiless heart could not appreciate the bliss of human affection.

It was in his study that his chief of confidence found him, and aroused him from gloomy meditation.

"Well, Dumilatre?" questioned Scarface, his eyes brightening.

"All is well in city and court, where the League continues to find adherents, and all the new recruits call on your grace to precipitate action. In the great drama of pretending to a throne, my lord, action is the only means."

"What else? I have the move ready, and it now depends on the king aiding me or becoming my obstacle! In either case I am resolved. What else, I say?"

The man hesitated.

"It is concerning the Lady of Cleves," said he. "The princess has been juggled with by the queen's soothsayer——"

"The queen's soothsayer?"

"Old Ruggieri, the Italian poisoner, who did the Queen Joan of Navarre to death. He is the queen's familiar spirit. Who knows what demons prompted them to entangle the newcomer from Germany, innocent as the dove, in their devices?"

"Entangle my bride-to-be!" cried the duke, playing with his dagger as he strode about the room. "Let them keep hands off. What have they done?"

"Administered potions to her. From my relations with Lady Sauve, the princess' chief lady, I learn that after putting her to sleep with a devil's draught, they conveyed her into the magical chamber of Ruggieri. Here, to assist in their designs, they showed her to a court favorite, one of the king's gallants, who has taken the place of Quelus, whom we killed by Antraguet's sword."

"A happy thrust! This court gallant, for whom they make my affianced one a raree-show, who is he?"

"He is the Count of St. Megrin, your grace."

"I scarcely know him."

"He is fresh from the country; but he is an accomplished swordsman, and the king engaged him as a favorite immediately on his trying his steel with the fencing masters."

"St. Megrin, eh?"

The valet took out of his satchel a small, exquisitely-cut glass flask of smelling-salts. The duke frowned, for he the more easily recognized this scent-bottle, as it was his present to his bride-to-be.

"It is the princess'—and was found in Ruggieri's rooms," said Dumilatre.

The duke knitted his brows.

"An accomplished swordsman," he mused, "but a mere gentleman compared with me! A combat, man to man, is out of the question. Dumilatre, go, get me those murderers who killed Duguast because he offended Queen Marguerite of Navarre. I suppose you can find them?"

"In some pothouse; yes."

"They would even beset a king's favorite?"

"They would beset even Lucifer's favorite, since they have had no employment of late, and hungry wolves respect no fleece!"

"Good! This St. Megrin will not long fill Quelus' place beside the sybarite prince!"

Dumilatre bowed, and was at the door when the duke recalled him.

"Let my gentleman-in-waiting prepare my

armor. I am going in full array to see the king about appointing the chief to the League."

He paused, and added, as if he desired Dumilatre to understand that he had not forgotten his tidings:

"On my return I will visit the princess at Soissons House. There must be an explanation of these magical tricks. I am straightforward myself, and do all things aboveboard!"

Dumilatre smiled, bearing as he did a message to employ secret assassins, but went his way in silence.

His lord, full of meditation, did not find the Louvre Palace gay.

The shadow, streaked with red, of St. Bartholomew's Eve, lowered upon it, and darkened every lobby and deep window recess.

The courtiers took their cue from the king, who sought quiet, and even the young men, his associates, alternately, in fantastic pastimes and extravagant devotional acts, shared the general dullness. Add to this that scarlet and purple were ranked as royal hues, and it can well be understood how monotony of the decorator's palette marred the interior. The bright paintings of the debauched Italian school had been removed from the walls or draped over when the king was fitfully fastidious.

The apartment called "Of the bath," because it had contained a "Susannah by the Bath," by Titian, was used as a secondary throne-room. There was no throne, but one end was slightly raised; upon this were placed two armchairs and several stools for the privileged to sit so near royalty.

The courtiers, principally those called "the king's gallants," being young and light-hearted, were playing chess, cards, and cup-and-ball, which was then a fad of the hour. They were named Joyeuse, Epernon, Halde, St. Luc and St. Megrin, the latest addition to their choice circle.

This Paul Stuart, Lord of St. Megrin, had the air of those angels with a sword which

Raphael tempered in copying them from Michael Angelo. His youth was so vigorous that he seemed five years more than twenty; his countenance was cherubic; his mustache was but down, and the blush on his cheek was pink and not red.

He came of a long line of warriors. "Not an ecclesiastic among us," had been his father's boast at a time when more progress was made by the prelate than the statesman, so that the aspiring statesman often became a priest.

He was graceful in every act, and yet all was so manly that he stood out like a stone man among wax effigies in the midst of the Valois' "gentle cutthroats."

A little melancholy, arising from his already looking seriously upon life, chastened the joyousness and impudence of his age.

He had that reserve of indefinable but valuable qualities found in captains of consequence, enabling them to save their company, if not themselves, in pressing situations.

He was a friend whom a companion could depend upon, a favorite who would not betray his monarch, and a captain who knew when to keep himself in the rear of his troops as well as to spring forward when the charge must be personally led.

Among the animated crowd in the apartment, St. Megrin was perhaps the only person who did not deign to join in the game of cup-and-ball.

"Bless us!" he cried, suddenly, amid this throng going and coming, and keeping the balls in the air until one was dizzy, "here is old Montprison!"

"The master of the ceremonies!"

"More like the master of the revels," said Joyeuse, between peals of mirth. "Hang me in chains, but he is playing with cup-and-ball, too!"

"One fool has made many," said St. Megrin.

"Oh, we are nowhere!" sighed St. Luc. "The

old marquis is ambidexter—he is keeping the ball going, with one in each hand!"

"Ha! ha! my tomtits!" chirruped the old whitebeard, in his cracked voice. "Methinks this is not so bad for a man of seventy!"

"Excellent! We acknowledge that you take the palm! But I cry a truce!" and Joyeuse fell into the royal chair, gasping for breath. "Here, boy, is a franc of gold. I have not so heartily enjoyed myself since I was a stripling and rode my first horse!"

"Now that you are composed," said the Marquis of Montprison, "I can, perhaps, get in the news?"

"Guise has fallen downstairs?"

"That sneak, Antraguet, has fallen upstairs again?"

"By St. Denis, you were never more right, Halde!" returned the ancient gossip. "That smell-feast has entered into favor anew!"

"That ram-scuttle! that traitor!"

"He is a traitor, for he holds with the Lorrainers."

"I do not doubt that," went on the tattler, "for his reinstatement in grace is due to the interposition of the Duke of Guise. The king is doing everything to please him now."

"Because he may need him and his bullies," said Epernon.

"Yes," said a soldierly-looking man, who was Captain Treigny, of the Queen's Guards, "for it appears that the King of Navarre is out-of-doors in battle array, casque a-top and spurs a-pied, galloping up and down and to and fro in front of our lines!"

"That beanpole of Navarre!"

"A great breaker of chains and lances!" returned Treigny, with professional pride in a born warrior.

"And is the Lorrainer to be the securer of our safety?"

"The worst of it is," remarked Joyeuse, wiping his brow with a perfumed handkerchief, "we shall have to fight before the cool weather comes. Fight in the false summer of St. Martin's! bah! Imagine riding out on a horse big as an elephant, with a hundred and fifty pounds of hammered iron on one's suffering frame, to come home brown as an Andalusian gipsy!"

"And down there, where they have all weathers at once!" added St. Luc. "It will be a scurvy trick to play on you wit-crackers at court, to decoy you out to crack your ribs with a stroke of the pike, and not a merry jest!"

"Ah, and since powder is made at home and no longer imported, every schoolboy carries a pouchful, so that a battle is no longer cuts and knocks, but singes and burns, a foretaste of purgatory! Why, I confess that I have more apprehension of a sunstroke than a sword-stroke! Ah, if I had my way, I would have all the fighting done as Bussy of Amboise fought his last duel—by moonlight!"

"Bussy! Ah, there is the bear-master to pit against the Bear of Bearne!" said Epernon.

"He is, indeed, one who must fight in the cool of the evening, though even then he could not be said to fight in cold blood. Where is that champion of the throne?"

"You know that he was banished?"

"Oh, what does Bussy care for banishment?"

"True, he refused to go, as usual."

"But, this time, look you, the King of Navarre urged it on his brother the Valois, because he made eyes at Queen Marguerite—as if we did not all do that! He defied that Henry, too, but his patron, the Duke of Anjou, prevailed on his liegeman, which Bussy is, to obey. He did so for the novelty of the thing."

"He is in Anjou beside the duke, being appointed his first gentleman-in-waiting," said Montprison.

"And very pretty cottage-burning, and way-laying, and crossing of swords and cudgels there is going on down there, where Bussy struts!"

"Good for the Guise, since it is one formidable antagonist the less!"

"Perhaps," interrupted St. Megrin, grimly, "there has sprung up another in his vacancy!"

No one perceived what he meant.

"It is evident that there will be no peace this side of the Rhine and the Pyrenees until the Duke Henry is wed——"

"Wed to that pretty dame out of Germany who is enveloped still with the fog, like Loreley of the Rhine?"

"No, till Guise is wed to the rope-maker's daughter!"

All stared at St. Luc, who vulgarly put it that the great duke should be hanged. They did not yet talk of hanging princes.

"Guise! Guise!" loudly exclaimed St. Megrin, with more warmth than the settled animosity warranted. "Will we never cease being dinned with the Lorraine warcry? Let the chance come for us to thrust and cleave and—" he snatched one of the pair of gloves he had stuck in his belt, and hacked it furiously to shreds with his dagger. "There, by St. Paul of Bordeaux! I would hew all these petty princelets of Lorraine into scraps like that!"

"Look out!" said Treigny, with contempt for such a boyish outbreak by a rustic noble fresh come to town. "The Scar-cheek carries a sword blessed by the Pope and welded out of meteor steel!"

"If he had St. Michael's blazing glaive, still would I vie with him!" said St. Megrin, to the general surprise.

"Vive St. Megrin!" uttered Joyeuse, in the silence, "have with you! I hate this domineering black-brow as much as you."

"That is impossible. I would give my rank of count to feel his sword upon mine own for just five minutes! But the chance will come— perchance——"

"Not for the want of praying; we all yearn for a rush at the Lorrainers!"

Halde had prudently withdrawn into one of

the windows. They heard him call out in surprise.

"Lo, he comes!"

Many rushed to the casements.

"Guise? The duke?"

"No, no. Our friend, Bussy!"

"Bussy of Amboise!" was the joyous and flattering cry which arose in the courtyard, and was taken up on the broad stairs and echoed in the anterooms.

CHAPTER II.

BUSSY OF AMBOISE.

Few heroes returning from a victorious campaign had been so heralded under that historic roof.

Who was Bussy of Amboise?

The representative of the duelist consummate of the age, when the great wars had absorbed all the fighting element and left only those rarities, courageous by temperament, who infringed all civil regulations and royal edicts by drawing swords and using them as well against the legal officers as the soldiers, the civil servants. It was the protest of one who would not be hampered by the devices of a bought peace, and who detested, moreover, "the war of entrenchments" which gunpowder had forced upon the generals.

He was strongly built, but beautifully

rounded; athletic pursuits had so perfected him that he could have carried off all the prizes in an antique contest, and, as for weapons of his time, his prowess was that of a professor, not merely an adept.

Englishmen called him "the matchless," the Spaniards said he was *"e vencidor no vencido,"* that is, "the unvanquished victor," and his brother nobles, as we have seen, thought him fit to pair off with the Duke of Guise.

He wore a storm-cap, or helmet, composed of black leather, bound with brass. Otherwise, his dress was the court gallant's, sumptuous and gay as compared with that which the king affected when in his mourning spells. He had a long sword, which almost touched the ground, though girded up. It was tied at the hilt with a preposterous knot of ribbons, which was a token of some admiring lady's delight in his being her knight.

He was reputed to be the cause of the King of Navarre's jealousy of his wife, and he was also accounted one of the reasons why the monarch should seek the papal dispensation to annul the marriage vows.

He walked in rather swaggeringly, under a perfect volley of cheers.

"Hail, our Bussy the Brave!—the adventurer!—the terror of his foes!—the glory of his lord!"

He bowed right and left, and touched his cap, which could not be easily removed.

"Yes, yes, gentlemen!" said he, in a full, rich voice, "I may be all that, but I am more surely the hope of my friends! I have returned among you."

"Good-day, luck-bringer!"

"What, St. Megrin! Have you been plucked at dice by coming to the court, as I urged upon you?"

"Why did you not write to me out of the desert, as you promised?" asked our gallant.

"Write in the stirrup? Oh, we have been ever on the move. Anjou is topsy-turvy with the Reformers displacing a thousand things that were thought settled. They agreed in each town that the church should be used alternately by both sorts of believers, and between them they burnt it down, and now each party, armed to the teeth, attends service under the canopy of heaven, at the opposite ends of the town!"

"So you were a hundred leagues off?"

"Three days ago, I was so. But I have not traveled by oxen-post." He looked down at his spurs and leather breeches and soft woolen hose. "I have had three goodish horses killed under me, by foundering. But here I am among my bottle-companions, after having rousing times with battle-companions."

"We feared," said St. Luc, "that the King of Navarre had slain you."

"Harry, good soul? Oh, it was by my pressure on Lady Sauve that he escaped from this palace when he was locked up with my own lord."

"And have you pacified Antraguet? He wanted to kill you as a tidbit for dessert after Quelus."

"Oh, Balzac? Antraguet and I met on the same road—that of banishment from court favor—and we had a fellow-feeling which passed the sponge over our enmity. We did measure swords, but found them the same length to a T. So we walk daintily when we meet, as if on 'foot-angles.'"

"The marquis says that Antraguet is restored to a hearing. Did the message of deliverance include you, Bussy?"

"No, Epernon; alas! no. But I must bear the Lady of Sauve the token of King Henry of Navarre's gratitude for her connivance at his flight. Has the king forgiven her?"

"Oh, he does not war upon women!"

"Well, he will have all the war with men that he has the appetite for," said Bussy, gravely. "They are getting into fighting trim in the south, and, this time, it will be action every day. I came back because—because I want to keep my hand in. Is there no street-fighting yet?"

"The streets are dull as the church-walk."

"No clash with the Guisards?"

"We rub up against them," said Joyeuse, sadly, "but it is impossible to knock sparks out of a wet mop!"

"I thought, as the king's blight prevents me appearing as a principal, that I might scratch the rust off by being a second in an encounter."

St. Megrin laid his hand on the gladiator's arm, and, feeling the muscles significantly, said, in a deep voice:

"If you do not quit us too soon, you may have that post!"

"It is not in the king's gift," sneered Bussy, to whom the weak Valois was antipathetic.

"Have you had no single-handed combats in the dales and on the meads?"

"Alas!" sighed the arch-Hector, "my renown was trumpeted before me, and spoilt all, like that flute player who played by order of the mayor before the classic hero. No one would pick up my glove. Nor," added he, looking narrowly and puzzled at the remains of St. Megrin's dilapidated gauntlet, "insult me by kicking it to pieces."

No one gave him an explanation, for the assemblage was very mixed since Bussy had brought in a host, and followers of the House of Lorraine might be among them.

"The swallow loved nature for making it most swift," repeated Bussy, who was accomplished in the poetry of the period, "but if it were less so, it could enter into more races."

"You have only to stay," said the count, steadily, "for it may be your reputation is a red flag to the bull out of the east!"

"So much the better!" exclaimed Bussy; "I am the man to lie perdu as long as the king is displeased, but I will come out at the mildest call to stand by you! So do not fail to accept any challenge for a fight where the second may also be dragged in. I have not had a quarrel once a week where I was. Luckily, when I was in a miserable state, my hand writhed up with cramps from non-use, up came our friend Pha-laire——"

"The rabid Protestant!"

"Oh, he is not rabid now. He is meek, if anything. We met three time—and a half—the half was when the city archers at Pau inter-rupted our strife."

"Did you fall out about a point of creed?"

"Why, no; we fell out about a point of or-thography."

"Bussy and orthography? Ha, ha, ha!"

"Yes; he maintained that a painter was right who put a dot between every word of a barber's sign, while I offered my blade to my argument that it ought to be a cross, or ought to be naught."

"You are a wise pair! Who could have backed you in such a dispute?"

"Who? Crillon, the ultra-brave, who was my supporter, though we differ in belief."

"How was it settled?"

"The painter settled it, by agreeing that the gentlemen should both be served. For the future he would leave a blank between the words—neither cross to please the old church nor periods to please the new! Besides, the man of pigment said that he was paid by the letter, and not by the space between.'"

One of the gazers at the windows interrupted by calling out, in the proud tone of one who had made a great discovery:

"Antraguet has had the breach filled up! He is coming. I spy one of his men in his livery."

Those at the casements flattened their noses at the tiny panes; others craned their necks over their shoulders; others still, stood on tiptoe to see over those in front.

"What a whirligig it is!" commented Bussy, twirling his mustache much as a lion switches his tail in anticipation of prey approaching.

"Who would have thought he could be seen here again, after his sending Quelus in morsels to his grave?"

"Poh! the over-ruler has solicited his forgiveness, and obtained it," said St. Luc.

"The over-ruler? Who is over the ruler, in my absence? The old lady (the queen)?"

"Bussy, it is the Duke of Guise, of course, never more mighty."

"Oh, yes! And they call me a bully? I, who never 'solicit' in his bull-baiting style! Ah, he is still more insolent and overbearing, our dear Lorraine, is he? Oh, dove that I am, and raven that he is! Ah, but the white and the black feathers will fly and get mixed, you will see!"

"To-day, red; to-morrow, white!" said St. Megrin, bitterly and with emphasis, in support of his brother-in-arms' threat.

Most of the swordsmen intimated by smiles and nods that they were opposed to this victor's return.

"Gentlemen." said Halde, "is it not written

in 'The Morality on Blasphemers': 'By our sharp and ready swording, we slay caitiffs and lording?'"

"Let the king study that text," said Joyeuse, "and when he preaches its inculcation, why, we will act upon it!"

"It is Antraguet! It is Balzac! He enters the courtyard amid a swarm of his compeers!"

"Oh, the king will not heed that uproar; he is deeply engaged in learning Latin."

"Latin?" repeated St. Megrin, "what need has he of a dead tongue to distress live gentlemen? He has only to say: 'This way, my nobles!' to have a thousand swords fly out of the sheaths where mold is sticking them. In these breasts is the same spirit, albeit smouldering, which enflamed the victors of Jarnac and Moncontour, and these odoriferous gloves have not too far softened the hands that they cannot hold the blades of their sires firmly!"

"God, excellent! to it, St. Megrin!"

"Yes, it is easy to make pipes when reeds are handy," Epernon jeered.

"But not so easy to make the Guisards dance to our piping," said Joyeuse.

"Hush, boy!" interposed the baron, holding up his hand, "for Antraguet is at the door!"

But the pardoned desperado had too much sense to walk in among his enemies without testing the ground. He had halted in the ante-chamber to confer with the functionaries about the king's mood.

It was a much more important personage that the tumult was about.

Epernon held up his hand, whispering:

"Hush, my boy; here he is."

There was a ranging of armed men against the walls without. A rustle of cloth of gold and chains, a shuffling of fine shoes, and the doors were thrown open in both panels. This was a royal entrance, and a page stood in the opening and uttered the talismanic words:

"Gentlemen, the king!"

Bussy alone removed himself from the rush to catch the royal eye. He thought it wise to keep a little apart. He would for once be prudent, and only disclose himself if the monarch was in good humor.

"I have played all my trumps," muttered he. "Only the king-card can raise me out of the dumps."

The cry was repeated in various quarters: "The king!" and the courtiers began to practise bowing.

In the thick of a glorious mass of color, metals, and laces, the King of France, and the queen-mother, entered the hall.

CHAPTER III.

THE THIRD HENRY.

The king took his seat, and the pages arranged his robes so that he should be at ease, for he was dainty as an invalid.

Under an ornamental cap, rather than crown, for his sick head could not long endure the weight of the gem-laden circles, his long face seemed doubly pale; his eyes were lead-lined, and conveyed the idea that he slept at unusual hours, and badly, at that.

He now and then plucked at his pointed beard, feebly grown, and redolent of pomade. His ruff was starched with the poor flour of the period, and, being yellow, not white, gave a cadaverous, green tinge to his artificially-ruddy complexion.

His hands were truly feminine, and exaggeratedly long, as if, in cracking their knuckles, which he did to contend with a tendency to cramp, he overstretched them.

He was the last of the Valois, which had had its culminating point in Francis the First, and declined with Charles the Ninth, dying with him under the knife of the fanatic.

Since he had reigned in Poland, he had shivering fits like a delicate lady; he returned from that kingdom, to take his brother's place on this throne, only four years anterior.

He gracefully returned the salutations of the glittering assemblage. It was even larger than commonly, as the news of Antraguet's return, after exile, and the belief that the Duke of Guise had a strong card to play, which the monarch hardly dared trump, set all teeth on edge.

"Greeting, nobles and gentlemen!" said he, in his sweet, lingering voice. "Villequier," said he, dropping his voice, "see if the tailor has brought me my new riding suit. Page, run to our queen, and let her know that I shall call in at her rooms, after this audience, for I am wishful to fix the date for our pilgrimage to Our Lady of Chartres, where we have a special prayer to offer; and, mark!" raising his voice, penetrating, though seldom forcible, "all are welcome who accompany us on that holy errand."

With the audacity of a pet page, St. Megrin, leaning on the arm of a reserved chair, lifted up his voice, saying:

"Please your majesty, what if you were to command a campaign into Anjou, in lieu of ordering a journey to the shrine of Chartres?"

"Ha!" ejaculated the old queen and her son at the same time, at this bold suggestion.

"Yea, into Anjou," repeated the favorite, with stress on each telling word. "If your followers wear steel jackets and iron caps, instead of ashes and sackcloth, and carry naked steel, instead of sputtering candles, your majesty will not lack for penitents; and your majesty will see the Count of St. Megrin in the foremost rank, though he had to make the rest of the road on bare feet over burning coals!"

There was a buzz of approval among the irreverent.

Henry half-closed his eyes to concentrate the rays as he glanced around. He eyed all the faces, as if he were willing to howl with the wolves, but wished to make sure that they were in the majority, as compared with the sheep. Then, coughing drily, he replied, as mildly as ever:

"There is a time for all things; let them take their turn. As soon as needs press, we are not going to lag—never fear, boy! But, at the present speaking, thank goodness! our fair realm of France is at peace."

Several composed countenances became drawn awry, for the intelligence that the rebels, under King Henry of Navarre, were mustering in numbers, as if, at least, to counterbalance the gathering of the Holy Leaguers, was diffused widely.

"We do not want for leisure"—he dwelt upon the word, very dear to him, for of all the sluggish monarchs it was he who most often had his lulls broken into—"leisure for our devotions."

As if only then he perceived Bussy among the faces at the back, though noticed at the start, he exclaimed, with well-pretended surprise:

"What do I see? the Lord of Bussy again at my court?"

Bussy swerved on his hot feet, not knowing whether to advance or retire, when the queen-mother spared him an anxious moment by giving him a smile, and saying, for him to overhear and prepare his answer:

"Nay, no doubt your brother Francis hast sent him with news sweet to your heart and mine, his mother's."

Henry imitated her smile, therefore, and said, pleasantly:

"So you have been wool-gathering out there

in the meadows. Ah, methinks you have spun little by it!" alluding to the steel cap, which showed some dents and grazes.

"I have left a lock or two on the briars," mumbled he.

But the king had turned to his mother.

"If your well-beloved son," said he, genially, but it covered a sting, "had been a submissive brother to me, and a respectful subject to his king, he had no need to be a fugitive from this court."

She lowered her eyes, to prevent him seeing a savage gleam, and replied, with suavity:

"Perhaps he comes with his respect and submission?" looking at Bussy to give him the cue.

"Well, we are about to know that—or something. Keep your seat, mother. You may come near, Lord Bussy! Where did you leave our brother?"

"In town, my liege."

"The dev—he has been in our good city of Paris?" and this time it was true surprise.

Others in the surroundings felt, and some expressed, the same feeling.

The French had not attained the barbarism of Turkish politics, by which, on ascending the throne, all kin near the sovereign are deprived of life or sight, in order not to be such continuous menaces as younger brothers were to Francis, Charles, and Henry.

"He only spent the night here," quickly continued Bussy.

"Merely passing through?" went on the questioner, jestingly. "Going home again?"

"Oh, no, continuing his route—to Flanders."

"You hear this, mother?" said Henry. "It looks to me as if our family will include ere long a Duke of Brabant. But, still, sir, how comes it that he skimmed by us, without stopping in to present his homage of fidelity to his elder and his monarch?"

The messenger did not want for temerity, but he shrank from giving reasons for his master's erratic actions.

"Faith, sire! he knows how dearly your majesty loves his brother, and he foresaw that, once under your hospitable roof, you would not let him go forth as easily as he departed the last time."

Alençon—for Francis of Anjou acquired the latter title from his brother Henry, on his having to relinquish it on becoming King of Poland, dignity excluding his retention of foreign appanages—Alençon-Anjou had been actually imprisoned in the Louvre with the King of Navarre.

"You are, my old Bussy, a blunt speaker," said the king, relaxing, for, timid himself, he admired such fearlessness, "and you do not 'cut' your wine with water! But you are right; that is, he is right." He made the grimace of a terrier which had let a rat escape from overconfidence. "But in the North he will be exposed to danger. At the moment, he must long for the presence of his good servitor and his best sword——"

Bussy bowed, but forefelt that the wind was about to whisk round unfavorably.

"He may need them both, to be used against us——"

"As I hope to live, no, no, sire!"

"Nevertheless," persisted Henry, though the energy of the denial stirred him, "you should arrange to leave us as soon as possible, and join him quickly!"

Bussy bit his lip and stepped back, his discomfiture intensified by seeing a gentleman in the Balzac-Entragues livery go by toward the king's chamberlain to present his master's name.

"There, there, what is it?" testily asked the king, scratched by his ruff, and plucking at it.

"My son," said the queen, as she saw the official hesitate, "that play-devil, Antraguet, is taking full advantage of the permission you voluntarily accorded him to reappear in your desirable presence."

"Ay ay, 'voluntarily'—hum!" repeated the

king, crisping up his somewhat drooping lip. "The murderer of my minions! of Quelus, the Incomparable! But living pearl is worth dead gold!" sighed he, seeing that he was watched to note how he bore this imposition from the Lorraine faction.

It was pressing him with a great sacrifice, that was manifest; but he clasped his hands, and mumbled a prayer of contrition.

"Speak, sir!" said he to the messenger from the offending courtier.

"I have the honor," began the gentleman, uneasy as a bee in a strange hive, "to say that Charles Balzac of Entragues, Baron of Dunes, Count of Graville, formerly lord lieutenant for the Government of Orleans, begs to deposit at your majesty's feet the homage of his respect and fidelity."

"Hem! I suppose," said the king, to his mother, "that we must be thankful that this firebrand slides in at the doorway, instead of hurling himself in at the window?" Aloud, he answered: "We will presently receive our faithful and respectful servitor. But let me, beforehand, divest myself of all that might remind me of that shocking combat, hand-to-hand." He rose. He beckoned to Joyeuse, who, with others of the select, had drawn near, as if to fall upon the envoy. "Here, my dear boy," taking from around his neck a sachet highly perfumed, and extracting some tokens, "here is a keepsake, indeed—Quelus' earrings! Wear them in memory of our departed friend."

Epernon followed Joyeuse at a similar beckoning.

To him he gave a gold chain of exquisite work, due to the "Unknown Pupil of Cellini;" and to St. Megrin, whose contempt for trinkets he already knew, a sword, which a groom of the chambers brought him, having it in readiness.

"This is the sword of Schomberg," explained he, with rare feeling; "it was heavy for a hand of eighteen years only! May it be better defended on the next occasion like that! Now, gentlemen," he resumed, quickly, to cut short their thanks, "like me, do not forget them in your prayers. Mine ever is:

" 'Schomberg, Maugiron, and brave Quelus, may they rest free from what assail us!' Remain near us, but be seated."

He gave this direction in order that their attitude should be less menacing, for his reminiscence had spurred them all.

He made a sign to the ushers and the master of the ceremonies, who proceeded to let the suppliant in.

"If they honor the Butcher's man with such pomp, what will they do for the Butcher?" muttered Joyeuse to his neighbor.

There was a deep silence as the Baron of Dunes marched in, very martial in bearing, for many a man entered a lion's den with less cause for dismay.

On seeing his favorites' slayer, the king inhaled smelling-salts like a woman.

If Antraguet perceived this incident, he did not show his contempt, for he knew that the scratch of this tiger-cat was fatal as that from a royal tiger's massive paw.

Although attired with splendor, the baron had his hair and beard cut and trimmed for wearing the close iron helm. He had let his boots fall, but they wore not the golden spurs, but steel ones, with immense Spanish rowels, such as became a horseman whose steed might alone save the master in a race for life. His sunburnt visage and undimmed eyes, spoke of the warrior who would prefer his exploits should be on the tented field, and not on the duelling-ground.

With a hand on his hip, beside his war-sword, he bore the scrutiny and the taunting looks of the minions, handsomely; but in his heart he quailed at the glances of the queen-mother. He was well cognizant of her hate for the Guises, and that he had been regarded, dur-ing the halcyon days of his enjoying the king's errant favor, as most active in preventing her swaying him into repulsing the duke and his brother.

It is needless to say, perhaps, that her hatred was "curdled affection," for she, the queen, had been very friendly with the old Cardinal of Lorraine.

Henry watched his enemy approach, and, as he wavered, made him an imperative sign to bend the knee, so that there could be no doubt about the obeisance.

"Charles Balzac of Entragues," spoke he, "we grant you the favor of our royal presence, in order that we may, in the midst of our court, restore you, in the place where they were removed from you, your titles and dignities. Rise, Baron of Dunes, Count of Graville, and Governor-General of Orleans, and retake beside our royal person the functions which you heretofore fulfilled. Rise!" reiterated he, for the noble remained kneeling.

"Nay, sire," explained he, "I should not rise

yet, nor until your majesty publicly acknowl-
edges that my conduct in that fatal duel was
becoming a fair and honorable gentleman."

This was rubbing salt, if not poison, into the
raw, but Henry, with all his faults, knew when
to bow to the inevitable.

He did it with grace, too.

"Verily, we will acknowledge that much,"
said he, "though your words are mortal as your
sword, for it is God's truth! Ah, but they were
terribly painful wounds you dealt!"

Seldom had the speaker been seen to wince
under such piercing anguish.

"Why, he loved them!" muttered Epernon,
amazed.

"Enough to avenge?" questioned St. Megrin, in a whisper.

But the baron would not reply in any way.
The other clutched the gift sword by the hilt as
if, like a certain fabled one, it imprisoned a
demon, and could answer by its voice.

"Would your majesty, therefore, deign me

your hand to kiss as gage of pardon and forgetfulness?" continued Entragues, as though pursuing a set formality.

The king shrank back in the high back of his seat.

"Forget it? Heaven! no, you must not crave that, sir!"

The old queen saw his favorite's eyes flash.

"What was agreed?" whispered she, nervously.

"Well, no," returned he, slowly, "I—I may pardon him, as a good Christian should—but forget! never will I forget it all my life."

Entragues rose at last, reluctantly saying:

"Sire, I appeal to time to come to my relief. Mayhappen, my submissiveness and my fidelity will finish with allaying your grace's wrath."

"It is possible. But—your government has need of your presence! It has been too long deprived of your services, and my subjects may suffer in consequence."

The noble frowned at the rebuke.

Fortunately, attention was called off him by a salvo of firearms in the streets, and an immense cheer rolled out of the St. Honore way, up to the palace gates, where the mob re-echoed it to the deepest note.

"What is that din in the face of the town?" inquired the king, apprehensive.

"It is," replied Epernon, guessing without looking out of the window, "the Duke of Guise leading the dance!"

"Oh, is he escorted by the rabble?" said the king.

He nodded to Captain Solern, of the arquebusiers, and to Testu, knight of the palace watch, who immediately quitted the hall to protect the entrances.

"Suppose I set the measure here? Our dear cousin of Lorraine does not, it appears, profit by the privilege of sovereign princes to enter our court unannounced! Always his attendants make turbulence enough for his arrival not to be a mystery."

"Only such 'mysteries,'" observed Joyeuse, "as the olden ones where the noise was thick about the devil."

St. Megrin bent forward so that he could speak almost into the royal ear:

"He acts toward your majesty like one power to a like power. Like you, he has his subjects, and I dare say that he will come before-fore you, armed to the teeth, to present a humble request!"

CHAPTER IV.

A RAPID ASCENT.

The assemblage became very compact, for a crowd of splendidly-appareled gentlemen and pages preceded the master and pressed back the royal servants. The nucleus of this inrush was the Henry who annoyed his namesake as much—because nearer at hand—as the other of Navarre.

St. Megrin had hit the center in his jest. The Duke of Guise was in full war harness. But his casque—a masterpiece of the armorer's art, chiseled and inlaid, and flourishing two or three immense plumes—was carried by a page; another held his truncheon as a general commanding in chief; and four more brought up the rear with their little daggers thrust naked in their belts. He was so lustrous in the shining steel that he eclipsed the most brilliant of the fops in gold.

His face glowed from satisfaction at the way
he had been acclaimed in his almost triumphal
passage, but it was marred by the famous scar,
which looked livid. From his shoulders depended a magnificent mantle, not lined, but
showing one self-color, yellow as gold and
with the sheen of silk, being "the prince's
color." On this cuirass striped several ribbons
of knighthood orders—black for St. Michael,
red for St. Louis', and a local decoration, his
by birthright.

Even St. Megrin could not deny that the
people had chosen a patrician, and that this was
the most kinglike personage in the apartment.

The king had donned his most inviting smile,
as had also the queen-mother. A wise man
would have preferred a less effusive reception.

"Come, my lord duke," said the sovereign.
"One who heard the approach of your fore-
runners and who divined you from afar, said
that he offered to wager that you came still

again on behalf of my people, to have abuses reformed, or a tax struck off?"

"Let the tongues wag!" muttered the duke.

"My people are a happy people to possess in my bold cousin so indefatigable a representative and in me so patient a ruler!"

Guise had not crooked the knee; his bend of the head might be excused by the gorget, but it was scarcely perceptible.

"It is true that your majesty does accord me boons. And I am proud of being the intermediary between the lord and his lieges!"

The provost of the merchants and three or four sheriffs who had accompanied out of the city, applauded him with a murmur.

"This is the falcon playing the go-between of the hunter and the game," remarked St. Megrin.

"But this day that is," went on the duke, "a more powerful motive still brings me before your majesty, for it is presented both in your interest and the people's."

There were some lowering looks, for most courtiers spoke less widely of the bounty emanating from the crown. "The people" was no watchword in the prince's mouth.

Henry gnawed his nails with some impatience. He foresaw that the business was serious, and he fretted at anything which long claimed his attention.

"If the matter be so serious, you cannot wait, I fear me, until the assembly of the Estates of Blois, which is at hand?"

Guise looked questioningly at the civic dignitaries, who urged him on.

"Thither the three classes will have deputies, who, at least, have duly received the commission to speak to me in the name of their mandatories."

This implied censure on the foreign prince who volunteered to meddle with home affairs did not check the duke.

"Your majesty knows that this meeting is merely to pass settled business, and will dissolve instanter, not to meet anew until November. When the danger is pressing, it seems to me, and others, that a Privy Council should be called."

"Hang it! look at him calling out the Privy Council!" said St. Luc, in an undertone.

"Oh, if there be danger, and if the said danger be pressing," said the sybarite prince, like one aroused, "you truly alarm us, my lord of Guise." He looked around with the growing smile of a player who saw more and clearly how to meet a dangerous move. "Well, I declare! All the usual members of the royal councils are in the presence."

His cluster of favorites smiled with him.

If they could not often applaud his bravery, they could his wit, with good grounds.

"You may, therefore, speak out, my lord duke! Speak!"

The queen rose statelily. She perceived that the tide was rising, and she never waded when she could induce some one to carry her over a flood.

"In the case of debate in the council," said she, "I beg to withdraw!"

"No, mother, no," said Henry, not cheated by her unusual modesty, and reasoning that her assistance was better than none, "the duke knows that we never keep back anything from our august mother, and that in more than one important matter her advice has been of the utmost utility."

Guise ceremoniously bowed to the queen, who wished to avoid committing herself, though the proceeding was cut and dried.

"Sire," resumed he, "the step I am empowered to take is bold—perhaps too bold—but to hesitate any longer would not be the proper act of a good and loyal subject."

"To the facts, duke, to them," said the king, growing impatient.

"Sire," went on the other, who had never made a longer speech than this which he had rehearsed, "immense but compulsory expenses have exhausted the state treasury—necessary, of course, since your majesty approved them."

"I approved the outlay, but not the spillage and pillage," commented the king, perking up as if an economical monarch like King Henry of Navarre.

"With the aid of faithful subjects your majesty has found the means of keeping the stream aflow. But this cannot run on forever."

"The deluge only lasted forty days," remarked the monarch. "The Pope's approbation had to be obtained to permit the alienation of two hundred thousand livres' income from the clerical property."

"It was like drawing a back tooth," still interpolated the hearer. "Parliament allowed a loan for expelling from the kingdom all foreign men-of-war——"

"They would have starved here, while now they are fattening at the expense of Spain."

"The crown diamonds——" proceeded Guise, without letting the criticism embarrass him.

"Lord! will not he let the crown diamonds alone?"

"They have been pledged to Duke Casimir."

"This man was born to be a trader. I wager that he knows the amount and the interest," said the king, under his breath.

"For three millions as security."

"He did know it."

"The sums intended for the city hall have been used otherwise, and the General Assembly of the Estates had the audacity to reply with a refusal, when your majesty offered to pledge the royal domains for a loan!"

"Yes, yes, I own that the finances are in a deplorable condition. As the old wives say: 'Begin in gain, in straw be lain.' We, cradled in fine linen, will sleep on a truss of hay. Money is not so much the root of evil as of scarcity. But we must change the manager of the treasury! Do you know of a sure man?"

"In peaceable times, any manipulation may postpone the evil, but your majesty is now constrained to embark in war."

"War? The bolt is shot!" moaned the king, as if overwhelmed.

War was his bugbear. This approaching struggle would be the sixth or seventh civil strife which had fatigued Henry, without its being utterly suppressed. Of all the many enervated rulers of France, he most heartily longed for inertia, and lo! as if in anticipatory punishment for his odd defects, his reign was the most convulsed.

Guise, as if quoting documents, presented a a long series of horrifying facts and surmises.

Encouraged by the indulgence of the king, the Huguenots had made dreadful progress— one general had taken one province, one, another; Condé was master of Dijon. Gascony and its neighbors were in revolt. Taking advantage of these dissensions, the Spanish had burst into Agen, where hundreds of houses were burning over the corpses of thousands of citizens, put to the sword.

Henry sprang up at the end of the recital.

"As there is a living King of kings!" said he, "this being true, we must chase the Huguenots out of the kingdom and the foreigner back into his own. We do not fear war, my fine cousin, for we have not shot off all our powder! If these devils drive, we will go to the tomb of St. Louis and snatch up his sword, to march at the head of our brave army with the old, victorious warcry of 'Montjoie St. Denis!'"

A loud burst of enthusiasm hailed this speech, which destroyed etiquette.

St. Megrin took advantage of this suspension of the rules to say, as one man to another:

"If it is that beastly money which is lacking, your nobility will return what, after all, flowed out of the royal bounty! Our lands, jewels, and bars in the chest can be turned into coin, my lord duke! and, with God our aid, by melting down the gold thread in our robes and the trinkets of our ladies, we can keep the air full of silver and gold bullets!"

"Do you hear that, my lord?" said Henry, without disapproving the young man thrusting himself forward as spokesman.

Guise looked furiously at him.

"I hear, sire. But before the idea came to the Count of St. Megrin, thirty thousand of your brave subjects felt it their duty. They have pledged themselves in black and white, under the cross, to supply the treasury with gold and the army with men. That is the aim of the Holy League, and it will act up to it when the moment sounds. But I cannot hide from your majesty the fears felt by his faithful subjects, while seeing that this great association is still not openly recognized."

He had come to the end of his address, and those who best knew the king doubted that he could answer him commendably, prologue, speech and peroration, as the scholars say.

"What should be done to quell such fears?"

asked the monarch, with the finest innocence imaginable.

The duke, falling into the trap, could not conceal the satisfaction with which he pointed to the field marshal's baton on the cushion, with which the bearer advanced.

"You have but to appoint the chief, sire—one of a great sovereign house, worthy of his confidence and trust by his birth and courage, and one who has, above all, afforded proofs of his being a good son of the church—in order to calm the zealous as to his behavior under trying circumstances——"

This was plain talking, with a vengeance.

"My lord, I see that your warmth for our royal person is such that you would spare us the trouble to seek very far for this chief. But"—here he glanced one of those sly looks at his mother, fully capable of appreciating this double-dealing, which he shared now and then with her—"but we will consider all this at leisure—at long leisure—my dear cousin!"

"Yet if your majesty would appoint in the interim——"

Guise felt as if he had caught an eel, instead cf a serpent, but unfortunately, eel or serpent, it was slipping out of his hold.

The hearer masked a yawn with his dainty hand, and, lounging in his chair, replied in a tired voice:

"My lord the duke, when we yearn to hear sermons we will appoint a Huguenot to retail them to us. Gentlemen, methinks this is quite enough time to devote to affairs of state, and we should think a little of recreation."

All faces of the court brightened and broadened.

"Let me see! that masked ball was for this night, by a happy chance. It will take the taste out of the mouth of gunpowder and the torch—the dance music. I trust that you, my cousin, and the ladies of your house will embellish the gala."

Guise scowled with such a strong muscular

twinge that his scar turned scarlet, and it seemed that the old wound had broken out afresh. But the hue darkened into crimson as St. Megrin, not a jot daunted by the importance of his butt, thrust out his finger almost to rap on the gleaming corslet and said, sarcastically:

"Your majesty may see that his highness, the duke, is already in a fancy dress—that of a knight-errant."

"The knight-errants were redressers of wrongs," replied the insulted noble, haughtily.

"Troth! this attire, my dear cousin," said the king, approving of his gadfly by using a similarly biting tone, "strikes me as rather heavy and warm for summertide."

"If he wore so much pride on his sleeve any longer, it would freeze in winter," said Joyeuse, anxious to shoot his arrow in.

"These are times, sire," answered the baited one, but addressing himself markedly only to the principal in the badgering, "when a steel coat is preferable to a silken one."

"Silk in your ears," returned St. Megrin, a little hurt at not being retorted to directly, "for your highness may hear another bullet whistle by them."

"When bullets reach me as I face them," replied the duke, proudly touching his scar, "here shows proof that I do not turn my head to avoid them."

Joyeuse picked up his air cane, which he had discarded for the cup-and-ball, and began to load it.

"We will see how you stand this pellet making a thoroughfare through your pouting chest," muttered he.

St. Megrin took the toy out of his hand, and they thought that he had disapproved of the boyish sport. But he leveled it at the mark and saying: "Wait! It shall not be said that another than I had the experience!" discharged a sugar plum at the breastplate, on which it rang before bounding off. "The reply is to you, now, my lord!"

The minions clapped hands. Others turned pale. The sheriffs gathered up their robes as if to run out. The duke put his hand to his dagger, and the captains of the guards and the constable darted forward to prevent the weapon being drawn.

"Perdition! am I to be toyed with by that glover's forket?"

So growled the duke, shaking off the hand a courtier laid on his sword arm.

"What are you going to do?" whispered one of his men. "Puff! to a sugar plum."

"Ha! you stagger under it," cried Henry, delighted as his forefathers at a tourney where horse and man were borne down by a charging chevalier. "Why, cousin of Guise, I should have believed that pretty piece of Milanese millinery were proof to a candy ball!"

The cue was to laugh, and the laugh ran round.

Guise quivered with the effort to repress an outbreak.

"Oh, you join in, sire?" he reproached. "Let them render thanks that we stand in your presence!"

He snapped his partly-drawn dagger of mercy into its sheath.

"Oh, let that stand apart," interposed Henry, quickly, as if events had turned exactly as he hoped, but dared not believe in. "Let our dignity rest. Act, my lord, precisely as if we were not by."

This was a terrible speech. From the mouth of a King Edward II. it would have been death to this Mortimer on the spot. Or, at the least, the favorites would have fallen upon the Lorraine's train, but the latter conjectured that he had lost his opportunity, and that he should have come in stronger force. But he could not let this slight pass, since it was abetted by the king.

"Would your grace permit me to stoop to this wait bait?"

"Oh, nay, my lord! But"—he made one of

those pauses with which, like an actor, he preceded his jests—"but I can lift him up to your
level."

All held their breaths.   St. Megrin's rash,
puerile deed had brought about an event which,
with the tang of unexpectedness, had savor of
its own in its object.

"It seems to me, lord chancellor, that in our
broad dominion of France we can find some fief
to endow upon our faithful Count of St.
Megrin?"

"You are the master, sire, to endow or to be-
reave.   But, in the meantime——"

"Stay, duke, and see it out.   We are not going to keep you waiting.   Count Paul Stuart,
we create you Marquis of Caussade!"

"But this is a duke, sire," said the chancellor.

"Count Paul Stuart, Marquis of Caussade,"
continued the king, fluently, "we make you
Duke of St. Megrin!"

"Whew!" said Joyeuse, shaking his head, "to

think that my shot might have brought down this beautiful brace of titles!"

"Fortune is hard to mount," observed Bussy, looking wide-eyed at the country noble so soon achieving this altitude, "but it is easy to ride."

"Now, my lord of Guise," said Henry, tranquilly, as if he had arranged preliminaries like a king-at-arms, and the two knights had but to tilt at each other, "you can reply to him, for he is your equal."

"I thank you, sire, I thank you," said St. Megrin, calmly, with a kind of gratification, as if one of his prayers had been materialized, "but I needed not this great boon, and, since your majesty does not oppose it, I wish to defy him in such a guise that there must follow fight or flight in dishonor."

"Flight!" reiterated Guise.

It was the cuckoo word which he had often heard from his few prudent partisans, and he was to hear it later. He was so quarrelsome that he seemed destined to go down under a secret stroke.

"Harken to me, king and peers: I, Paul Stuart, Lord of Caussade, Count and Duke of St. Megrin, unto you, Henry of Lorraine, Duke of Guise! Be ye witness, all ye present, that we defy you to mortal combat, you and all the princes of your house, be it with sword alone, or sword and dagger, to the uttermost, so long as heart beats in the body and the blade clings to the hilt! We renounce any appeal to mercy, as we hold ourselves bound not to grant the same! On this, God and all the saints, with my patron St. Paul to the front, be my aid!"

He flung down at the duke's feet the fellow glove to that he had cut to patches, and added:

"To you and yours, one down—the others come up!"

"Bravo, St. Megrin!" cried Joyeuse.

"Handsomely tendered, that challenge!" said the Moontjoye king-at-arms, as a judge of the delivery.

"He dances well to whom Fortune pipes," commented Bussy. "If he chooses me as second, I could pair off gratefully with that ugly Antraguet of his!"

The duke pointed to the glove, for one of his adherents to pick it up.

"One instant, gentlemen," interrupted Bussy, unable to resist the impulse at the ball being set rolling. "Allow me to put in my say, your majesty! I, Louis of Clermont, Lord of Bussy in Amboise, declare here that I am brother-in-arms of the Count-duke of St. Megrin, and, as such, am his sworn second! I offer to fight to the uttermost likewise, to whomsoever stands forth as second to Henry of Guise, and as token of defiance and gage that I will be on the ground, I throw down my gauntlet!"

His glove fell beside the other.

Dumilatre, the duke's master-of-horse, hesitated between the two.

"Ho, ho!" laughed Joyeuse, whose voice lost all its languor and the treble distinguishing it

In usual conversation when he came out fore-most in the front of war; "Bussy, you have come back to rob your old companion of the honor to be next to St. Megrin! You are so swift that you give one no time. But rest easy; if you are laid low, I will thrust in and not thrust in the air!"

If King Henry did not relish pitched battles, he was fond of these duels, which were corners of a battlefield in miniature. He looked on the fire he had kindled, and which was spreading, much as the Roman may have gazed on his capital enflamed.

"Take them all up," said Guise to his old aid-de-camp; "ah, he was too late in challeng-ing me, let me tell you—for his doom was fixed before this day!" Then, looking round, he be-trayed that it was his power that had forced Antraguet upon the king's circle anew, for he singled him out by name.

"You be my second," he said. "Look ye, gentlemen," he continued for the general ear;

"I am playing for high stakes—I offer you your revenge for scaring off Quelus! Dumilatre, get ready my battle-sword; it is just the length of that bilbo which the fire-new duke inherits from little Schomberg!"

"You are right, sir duke! This is a battle-sword, too, and it is not in a boy's grip this time—it may pierce even that fine cuirass, so prudently solid! But I would cry for the combat to be with us stripped to our shirts, so that all could see whose heart beat the quickest!"

This expression was not uncommon when duelists were accustomed to take occult advantage of one another by wearing charms under their vests.

"Enough, gentlemen," said the king, beginning to smother the flame, under his mother's rebuking glance. "We will honor the combat with our presence, and we will fix the day to-morrow."

Henry's "to-morrow" would have seemed a blame to any but those who felt that this time he longed to see the blood of his *"after-konig"* pretender to his throne.

"Now, each of you, being a king's fighter, is entitled to a boon, and you shall be given it, now, not to-morrow"—seeing that his habitual word had elicited smiles; "what do you call for, St. Megrin?"

"Equal partition of sunlight and firm ground! The rest I leave to my God and my sword!"

"Schomberg's unappeased manes will fortify that! What does the duke desire?"

"The formal promise that, before the action, your majesty will recognize the league and appoint the leader. I have no more to say."

The citizens' representative bowed in the same appeal, intimidated, however, by their visit having clashed with this challenge.

"Although we did not expect this demand," said Henry finally, "we will conde—that is, consent to the request. Gentlemen, since the Duke of Guise has marred the sport, and we cannot well dance in a mask on the eve of another sanguinary duel, we will hold a council of state in the stead. I convoke you all, my lieges. As for the two champions," added he, changing his clear, incisive voice to a whining one, which he must have imitated from the worthy Father Gorenflot, the preacher of the Abbey of St. Genevieve, "I urge them to profit by the interval to think deeply of their souls. Break up the court, lord chamberlain!"

CHAPTER V.

IN THE ROLE OF CUPID.

All over fashionable Paris where the sad news had not been carried that, on account of serious altercation in the king's presence and with his acquiescence, the masked ball would be postponed, there was considerable flutter. Since tourneys were abolished, spectacles in which dancing and posing, for the stately *pavanes* were little else, were in vogue.

In Soissons House the commotion was intense; from the ladies and the guest, the Princess of Porcian, to the humblest servant, the maids participating in the toilets, and the footmen donning their best to escort the party, a fever was flushing the cheeks and brisking up the limbs.

The dressing-rooms of the Countess of Montafix, mother of the Countess of Soissons, and

her daughter were not capacious enough, and
the apartments assigned to Therine of Cleves,
including her oratory, were added to the suit,
with which they corresponded. Through the
ample doorways, the folding panels drawn back
and the *portières* gathered to the side, there was
an incessant flow of the dressing-maids carrying the splendrous attire, gorgeous appurte-
nances and heirloom jewelry.

Therine, Princess of Porcian, was in a wrapper screening her contour, but its elegance was
still betrayed by the undulations, as she walked
with the majestic tread of superior women who
have been reared from childhood in the inflexi-
ble iron framework entitled a corset. Her
usually placid, yet often animated countenance,
was clouded by some annoying sentiment, for
she viewed the objects of attire and adorn-
ment with inattention, though seeking something in the mass.

The page playfully took shelter behind her,
crying out with affected trepidation:

"Rescue, fair mistress! and protection, against the ire of your first attiring-woman!"

"What have you been doing wrong this time?" answered she, distractedly. "Still a mischievous act?"

"No fear for that, madam. I am a discourteous page, for I have too good a memory for deeds in which ladies were concerned!"

"Your ladyship seems thoughtful?" said Lady Cosse, affectedly fond of her charge, over whom she had been set by the queen-mother.

"Why, no; it is a trifle! but it was a keepsake. One of my mother's gifts. My little flask of pungent salts has become detached from my girdle-chains. See! has any one come across it?"

Everybody shook their heads, but promised willingly to keep a sharp eye for the missing bauble.

"I will hunt for it," said Arthur, "and my reward shall be that you will beg me off from Lady Cosse's choler!"

"Well, it does not deserve a high recompense, but it is dear to me. Proceed with your search, Arthur."

"If it contained honey-wine he would not be long finding it!" said Marie.

"And if it were shut up in the wise monks' books of 'The Art of Verifying Dates,' Lady Crosse would never light upon it!" said the boy, ducking his head to pass under the old dame's arm.

"Madam," said the maid, "while your highness was in her own rooms, there came in the Queen Louise, who wanted to show the darlingest little monkey that ever came out of the wilds of Brazil."

"Monkey to the contrary," said the elder dame, "she came just to spy about and discover what disguise her highness was to wear. She has been to Lady Montpencier's, I was notified, and I am much mistaken if she will not gather the points of all the masks and costumes of grand dames and great lords at the ball!"

Arthur had made a perfunctory scrutiny, and, returning to listen to the small talk, sat himself on a hassock at his mistress' feet, as she took a chair at the toilet-table.

She lowered on him a deeply wistful eye.

"I could see no flask anywhere," said he, not understanding that the bottle left at the alchemist's could become important.

Lady Crosse rattled on, as if to anticipate the royal lady Louise's budget being opened:

"The Viscount of Joyeuse is going to appear as Alcibiades, a Greek chief—his helmet is of carved molten gold, and run him up to a ruinous figure. His entire dress will cost ten thousand livres!"

"The Baron Epernon," added Marie, not to be outdone, "is to be another Greek—the Emperor Caligula, who comes in on a hobby-horse, with a head like nature, carved in ivory——"

Luckily, the little commentator, Arthur, was absorbed in his own thought, like a boy had chosen his own beau ideal or rather, ideal beau, and he exclaimed with enthusiasm:

"And how is the Count of St. Megrin to be dressed, Lady Cosse?"

The princess appeared to have been pricked with a pin, for she carried her hand abruptly to her neck, and held it there as to repress something which rose in her throat.

"Ah, the new favorite? Let me see—what was said about this chevalier out of the Bordelais, who might have come out of the witchwoods where Charlemagne's knights defeated dragons and other devourers of persecuted maidens? He was to have a most dazzling coat, but, though fresh from Genoa, he hastily countermanded the order, and the seamstresses toiled all night to finish the complete habit of Nostradamus, the star-gazer, something like our diviner, Cosmo Ruggieri, wears when the court favors him with a call."

"Ruggieri," breathed the high lady from the

Rhine border. "Does not this Ruggieri dwell somewhere in our neighborhood?"

"Close, indeed; but, since there is no communication of late years between this new mansion and the old one, which he hired, one has to go mightily roundabout! But, as the crow flies, it is only a stone's cast to——"

"You never spoke more truly!" said the page. "With a popgun I have sent a marble spinning into the brass tube which he thrusts out of his shattered window there, and by which he sees what the man in the moon is guilty of!"

Therine shuddered at this proximity, which explained partially her quandary.

Guise's spies had seen clearly; she had been drugged and transported by a secret way into old Soissons House, where Ruggieri had his laboratory. She had but a dreamy recollection of St. Megrin appearing to her, speaking with her and fading away—rather than walking—at an alarm: after this she had returned to slumber.

and, as said, all seemed a vision. Now, it must be accepted as a happening not to be contested.

"I tell you," said Arthur, a pretty page, "that the Count of St. Megrin, although newly come to court, cannot have found a flame—otherwise he would wear the lady's device on his sleeve."

"This young man might be cautious!" remarked the princess.

"A southerner!" said Marie, with contempt for such judges. "Cautious!"

"But pray," said the elder waiting-woman, "what is there so notable about this stranger that this boy makes him the object of his trumpeting?"

"Remarkable!" repeated the page, wounded, "why, he is the most promising gallant of the king's swarm, now that Quelus, the great swordsman, is dead, and that Bussy, the first after him, is out of favor! Why, I should ask nothing better of my good saint, than the honor of being his page, if I were not enjoying the grace of being the Princess of Cleves'!"

He kissed his mistress' hand, hanging list-less by her side.

"You like him?" said Lady Cosse? "What has this Count of St. Megrin done under your own eyes?" asked her mistress.

"Why, you know that, under the arcade by the Louvre, the dealers in toads and tortoises for the gardeners, and seeds for cage birds, and in birds themselves, have established a line of booths to amuse the loungers——"

"I know them, because they are so much in the way! I have had to turn out in my litter for them——"

"Well, I stopped to learn what had gathered more than ever a dense throng. A gentleman had thrown down a handful of silver, and was opening some cages with his own hand!"

"Oh, setting free birds! That is quite worthy of a saint——"

"It was a saint's act, for the gentleman was our St. Megrin."

"Your St. Megrin, if you please! All out of humanity?"

"Well, that may be—only, they were black-birds, and he said: 'Now, they may go back to Lorraine—we do not want any Guises in Paris —even one is too many!'"

"Guises? blackbirds?"

"The coat of the duke's house shows the blackbird, does it not?"

"Silence! for you have conjured up our— blackbird!"

Indeed, there was at the street gateway one of those appalling shouts which hail the passage of a popular favorite; intermingled roars of "Long live our Henry! Guise forever! Lor-raine, a Lorraine!" rose thunderingly.

"*Tacit!*" said Arthur. "It is not right that you should hear the little fool's bells tinkle any more when that great alarm bell booms! I'll be off!"

"Arthur, stay with me! I believe he is com-ing to me, not to confer with the old countess!"

Arthur ran to a peephole designed to give a view of any one crossing the courtyard. He turned his face round, and it was pale.

"It is your lord," said he; "he is in bright armor, which would do for a ball, but he looks grim!"

"Black will take no other hue!" said she. "Mind that you do not quit me until I order you!"

This was her first order which gave him qualms. The town talk ran, and he was, we see, a receptacle for it, that Guise could give the Prime Devil odds at villainy and beat him.

"But, bah!" said the little fellow, stiffening his upper lip, "the ball has not come off yet! It is the one with luck who brings the bride home!"

The next moment the duke entered the apartment.

CHAPTER VI.

OFFERING THE CUP.

"Ha, you are up!" said the Duke of Guise, fixing his eyes upon Therine, Princess of Porcian, after a cursory glance about the apartment. "Were you going to enter your dressing-room?"

"I was not, my lord, but I was on the point of calling my tiring-women to dress me."

"It is useless, lady, for the ball is not going to take place."

"The ball is put off!" said she, but truly it was not with the sorrow of most belles in her position.

"Small wonder that you are not very much distressed, for I see that you would have gone against your will."

"I do little with my will; I was in this event following your orders, and did what I did, not to let you perceive that they were painful to me."

"Do not ask too much of mortal man," he gruffly said. "I must say that your retiring mood, whether due to your being brought up among those Puritans, the Rhinelanders, or not, is absurd in this country, above all in this city, where is the court and wealth. Personages of our altitude are bound to show ourselves, to keep our name prominent and give our varletry an excuse to batten upon us! Why, we have abbesses in our family, but they do not go out in receptions, galas and ceremonials in full attire and insignia, too! You must show yourself at court, my lady, for persons inimical to your affianced one, notice your unaccountable abstention and comment spitefully upon it. Bring criticism on yourself if you must, but not on the family to which you are right soon to be allied! Come, come, princess of a Rhenish principality is only even with my sovereign dukedom! However, enough on this matter— I have another to discuss with you. Ah, that pest of a boy lingers here!"

"He is not a pest—he is a relative of mine!" said Therine, steadily.

"Arthur, begone!"

The boy presented a firm mien, and did not lower his eyes.

"Why should you banish the youth who is but Propriety, as I understand such matters? What makes you consider that we can have secret interviews?"

This was her first remark indicating that hostility might be up her sleeve.

"Why should we be burdened with him?"

"He is not an eyeservant!" said she, keenly.

"He may be an earwig, though!" sharply rejoined the duke, making to the page a most imperious gesture. "Do you fear to remain alone with me?"

"Why should I fear that, or anything, in the house of the Countess of Soissons and of her mother, Lady Montafix, they being of the queen-mother's circle, my patroness?"

He showed impatience; this was the first time

that she had uttered any kind of threat, and
one based on the growing enmity which he believed lately the old queen entertained for his
line, if not himself individually.

"In that case," exclaimed he, brutally turning on the page, "you be packing, wren!" He
walked almost over to him, without the boy
budging, although he winced. "Well, little
rebel?"

"I am waiting for my mistress' orders, my
lord duke!" replied the sturdy youth.

The princess shuddered to see how heavy in
the jaw the prince was with discontent. He
was capable of letting his gloved hand fall on
that peach-bloom cheek.

"You hear this, lady! How he trumps me!"

"Arthur, leave the room!" said she, reluctantly.

"I obey you," replied the youth, but he
stalked out very saucily, muttering: "After
all, he has not made me look blue!"

He was red. in fact.

It was a very feeble barrier, but the lady felt at a loss when she had no longer even this protection. As the duke turned toward her, baffled at this evasive withdrawal, she was taken with a nervous spasm; her high forehead was creased by a wrinkle like the cord of her ornament, called after the originator, "*La Ferronière*," and her mouth was contracted with disgust and vexation. But she soon overcame her feelings, and let her features recover the resignation common to the young women of her times, oscillating between cloister and boudoir, almost as chilling and dismal.

She knew well that she was but the living pledge of the agreement between her father and the house of Lorraine, concerning the succession to the duchy, which, extending on both sides of the Rhine, was of great strategical value. To be held as a pawn, more and more irritated her.

For a sulky air, there was little to choose between either of them.

The duke stamped his foot, heavy with armor, .as the door swung to with provoking slowness.

"It strikes me as strange, lady," grumbled he, "that my orders should require confirming by any one! your approval——"

"The youth is my man, and ought to look only to me!" she replied, sullenly.

"He needs whipping-cheer! but—this thwarting me is not becoming—is not warranted! Henry of Lorraine is known, and it is known, likewise, that his hands and his poniards force his commands!"

"You exaggerate! What consequence can you draw, my lord, from the waywardness of a child?"

"I? None! But I had need of his absence to transact private business. Have you any objection to be my secretary for the nonce?"

She persisted in her sudden mood of sarcasm, for she observed:

"Secretary? Is the warrior of the Lorraines become what we call a *feder-fechter?*"

"I can use both pen and penknife at my wish!" replied he, more and more surprised at this complete alteration in her reception.

"Why should I handle the pen for your lordship?" asked she.

"To write——"

"To whom—my father?"

"What does it matter? You should learn to follow my dictation!"

"In faith?" He did not like the knitting of her usually unruffled brow in determination. He had intended to direct her to sit at a writing-table, but he reconsidered this display of authority, which seemed defied, and himself brought paper and the ink dish, in which were stuck quills, to the table where she sat. He brushed away the toilet articles, with shocking indifference to their importance in a lady's eyes.

"Is there anything else you need?"

"I am sorry to say that my hand is unsteady."

He had seen that and reasoned that he had terrified her at last. "I fear that I cannot shape a character creditably. Let me ring for some one better qualified—for the honor!"

"No, lady; it is indispensable that it should be your hand!"

"Then, no one who knew it—and there are next to none here in Paris—would recognize it, for my hand still shakes like an aspen leaf!"

"I dare say it will be legible! Write——"

"At least, I would hear what you want written——" She took up the pen, as if beaten.

She was much surprised at the words spoken, and her face set hard:

FRIEND OF THE KING:—This night, members of the treasonable body called the Holy Union meet in old Soissons House, in the part inhabited by the Italian wizard. It is impossible for a stranger to enter among them by that way, but there is a secret entrance from Soissons House, through the apartments of the Princess of Porcian and Cleàvev——

She started. How much did this sinister betrothed of hers know?

"Write!" said he.

"I will write not a line until I learn to whom this is addressed——"

"You heard—to a friend of the king!"

"It must be a jest, for you are——"

"A friend of the king."

"But you are chief of this league!"

"Still, the best friend of the king in trying to rid him of the worst of his parasites!"

"It is a prickly jest—I will not handle it!" She threw down the quill.

"But if you hear to whom the errand is given!"

"You would not betray your own party—this is a deathtrap! Lead your quarry into it yourself, my lord! I shall not endanger my conscience—not stain my honor!" She rose.

"Your honor?" sneered he. "Who ought to be more guarding of that than your affianced? Let me be the judge of what concerns that— you as well as me! and write!"

"Your desire alone might command me— your command is not, methinks, yet authorized by any law of man or Heaven! I am bound to refuse such writing in the dark!"

"This is my order, order—do you understand? Obey!"

"At least, I have the right to inquire the cause!"

"The cause! All this mincing and brangling convince me that you well know that."

"It seems to me that you are not my king—not the King David, and that I am not your Captain Joab—Antraguet, to deceive by an Uriah—better change your secretary, my lord! I dismiss myself from the post of shame!"

He withered under her high and scornful look.

"You must write this letter!"

"You are speaking to a princess! Allow me to hear no more of this!"

He intercepted her, and it was plain that, inconceivable though the roughness was, under this roof, to a foreigner of rank equal to his

own, he would go to any length in this overbearing passion.

"You shall not depart!"

The wall of steel was impassable.

"You will obtain absolutely nothing from me
by compelling me to stay!" she answered,
firmly.

He imposed on her so by a movement of his
gloved hand that she settled down in the chair,
though her impulse had been madly to flee.

"You will find it more wise to reflect," said
he; "my orders, if scorned by your highness,
are not so treated by anybody else in Paris! In
brief, I could substitute for the drawing-room
and elegant oratory of the Countess of Montafix the humble cell at a nunnery!"

"If I must be retained here until I shall have
communicated with my father," returned she,
trying to show more defiance than she felt,
"name the nunnery to which I should retire!
If this is a question of raising money, for I hear
that you are levying to constitute an army—

pray believe me that the Princess of Porcian's estate can liquidate your charges on the dowry of the proposed Duchess of Guise!"

This was almost the outbreak of hostilities.

"That would be but a feeble expiation if such losses can be gauged in money! Besides, hope would follow you up to the convent gate—and perhaps slip in at the bars! There are no walls that it cannot overleap, especially if assisted——"

"Assisted—why pause——"

"Assisted by a ready, skillful and impudent hand——"

"Hand of my page?"

"Not so much a page's as a knight's."

"It is true, if times are not altered, a persecuted princess should find a knight!"

"Ah, do we meet on the same ground now?" His sparkle in the eye was not of delight, unless a sanguinary kind.

He shook his head. He was not going to play into her intention in this manner. Afraid that he would not be the victor in the parley, he returned to the former contest.

It was more in his element, being brute strength.

"We must begin that letter!"

"Never, my lord, never!" articulated she energetically, more pronounced than heretofore.

"Do not drive me to the end—it is too much that I should have threatened twice without once striking!"

"To obeying your insensate behests, I prefer the reclusion! ay, if eternal!"

There was too much of the martyr—for affection—in the stubbornness not to enflame his rage.

He swore one of those great oaths which great lords reserved for themselves. and they would have been surprised to hear from a vulgar youth.

"Do you imagine that I have no means to control you?" hissed he, bending over her.

"What other have you?" said she, with bitter ridicule.

The words had not died on her lips before her lips became cold and white. He had drawn from his breast, not the poinard with which he had menaced her, but a small, cut crystal phial which she recognized, as well by its unique shape as by the fragment of gold chain still around its neck, as her missing vinaigrette. Then he had found it, where she must have lost it, in the room of Ruggieri; or the latter had betrayed her and he knew all that had happened there.

She became marble, and listlessly watched him pour some fluid out of the bottle into a cup of water on the table.

It was not the aromatic salts—it was clear, but having the deadly promise of some limpid extracts.

She believed that he would not shrink from assassinating her.

"What would you do?" gasped she.

"Nothing! This is simply a beverage of which the bare sight should furnish a virtue not in my words!"

"Do you suppose——" she began.

"We are beyond suppositions," said he, sternly; "or—will you write at my bidding?"

"No—God have mercy on me!" She clasped her hands, as if nothing should induce her to take up the pen.

He offered the cup. A kind of essential oil floated on the surface, seethed slightly, and, permeating all the water, disappeared as if nothing had been added. If poison, it was such a sublimation as few less than Ruggieri in chemical acquirements could have furnished.

"In Heaven's name—for the relief of your soul, do not do this deed, my lord! I am innocent of any fault to merit this crime! Do not let the death of a poor soul, far from home and fatherland, sully your fame! Guise, this would be a pitiable, frightful misdeed, for I am guiltless as the Paschal lamb! See!" She fell at

his feet and bowed her head so that her loosened golden tresses swept the dust off his *cuis-
sards* and his iron-shod feet. "What do you
seek more than this humiliation?—worse than
you could make the peasant-born suffer! A
princess sues for you not to commit murder!
Fie! though innocent, yet I fear death—consider, I have seen so little of life!"

"I am not one to snap and miss!" said he,
with the grimness which had daunted many a
foe, and which repelled many a friend. "You
know the means to have this draft emptied out
vainly!"

CHAPTER VII.

THE "URIAH" LETTER.

The remedy was more dreadful than the bane. She had divined very clearly, and she was sure, since the smelling-bottle had returned under her sight, but replenished with the drug, that, through her, the Count of St. Megrin was aimed at. Certainly, he might enter the wolves' repair to learn the nature of the plot against his sovereign, if such a lure were sent him, but, though on the face of it there was nothing to incriminate the writer, she would not thus have decoyed a stranger to his destruction. She tried to believe that this was an experiment to test her courage; that even the duke, however cruel in open warfare, would not have a solitary enemy thus butchered in a conclave of cut-throats. She did not yet suspect the whole of his malignant and unheroic plan.

"Guise and Lorraine could not harbor this

execrable design!" said she, offering to rise, as if the comedy were over.

"Play?" he said, scornfully, with such a face that she cowered again; "it is a play where I throw not money but the man!"

He sought the life of a rival, therefore! His smile was so bloodthirsty that she hoped no more from her eloquence. She lowered her head into the cup of her hands, became like alabaster, and prayed a deep, silent prayer, without heaving of the bosom or swelling of the throat with sobs—the communion of a creature with its Creator. Any but he must have been abashed at being the intruder into this sanctuary of a human soul in conference with a higher power.

He did not bid her cease—he dared not. Never had he so dreaded that a chosen thunderbolt might pick him out and strike him. He shrank as she rose, not to try to escape, not to gain an instant, but ready—almost rushing on her death without the least appeal to pity.

She might be guilty of loving contrary to her vow of engagement, but she would die like a princess. She was so decided that she darted out her hand and clutched the cup.

"And the health is to marital obedience!" said he, ready to dash the liquor from her lips, though.

"To death!" replied she.

He writhed, for he saw by her last smile that she hoped to meet another in the world where there is promised no parting! He knocked the cup out of her grasp, and it was bent as it struck the floor; the contents splashed over the kitten, and it fled with a painful squeak. Its hair, scorched as by fire, bristled, and at each tip stood a bead of charcoal! What agony she had escaped!

He saw that she loved that other, and preferred him with death than the life of union with the affianced tyrant. He cursed him and her. He the more, because he was so profoundly loved. He could wish at feeling his inferiority to this duke of a day that he had swallowed that draft of anguish.

Scarcely able to contain himself from striking her to lie at his feet again, he grasped her by the hand and his heavy grip seemed to sink deep. In the circle of the steel plates which mailed the back, her arm appeared like a dove enveloped in a glittering boa's folds.

She uttered a low scream, more in horror at such a rude usage than for the pain.

"Write!" said he, dragging her to the table.

"You hurt me, sir!" said she.

"Write, I bade you!"

He felt through the leather that he held something more like marble than human flesh; the hand was like Parian, the arm above was congested with blood. He saw the veins clogged, like red lines on a map. With this shiver of cold, she had a mist creep over her sight. Then she smiled with a kind of thankfulness which he did not at the first comprehend—she was simply grateful because she thought that she was escaping his unmanliness and his cruelty by dying.

He released her, fearing that it was too late.

"Is she dead?" muttered he, as she sank to his feet. "No; it is one of those swoons which artful women call to their aid when there is no shield but insensibility for their confusion and their shame!"

On the enpurpled arm, the grip-marks became white.

"I would that band were around *his* throat!" said he. "Ah, beautiful women are like the deer—they would be hacked but for the gashed hide fetching the lower price!"

He sat down with pretended tranquillity, watching her as a duelist might one with whom, on coming to, a second and perhaps differently ending bout must ensue. He did not feel victorious.

He let her revive, without the least attention, hating and yet admiring, for she had braved death. It was physical pain which had vanquished her. Strong men had not in the rack, borne more without succumbing.

She sat up; she looked immediately at her bruised arm, and not at all at him; she drew her sleeve down upon it, and bound it with a strip of handkerchief. She rose—all without deigning a glance at him, and, standing unsteadily at the table, close to him, repaired the disorder with a studied ignoring of him which affected him more stingingly than if she had struck him with the flagellator's scourge of many strings.

"Well may you hide what you brought on you by your obstinacy!" he could not refrain from saying, in the irritation which this conduct caused.

She rang a handbell with her other hand.

"Write!" said he, persisting.

"If I were to write, it would be an inquiry what the nobility of France and Germany will say when told that the Duke of Guise had bruised a lady's arm with a battle-gauntlet!"

He would have replied, but Lady Cosse entered at the door, which Arthur had opened at the first tinkle of the bell.

"I was careless," said the princess to the old dame, who looked her surprise at the unusual animation of her mistress. "I overturned a cup, which has broken and cut me with the splinters. You will let me leave you, my lord?" she added, with freezing politeness.

She crossed to the door without hurry, nursing one arm in the other, and quitted the room without the usual ceremonious bow to her guest or host, for he had acted more like the latter.

The tiring-woman stared in consternation at the duke. Even her purblind eyes could see that this was something more momentous than a tiff between an engaged couple.

The Duke of Guise had taken off the glove which had left its ineffaceable mark on that spirit, if not on the arm, and looked as if he could have stamped it out of shape. He laid it on the table, and said, in a broken voice:

"Do not follow your lady."

He wrote the lines which he had dictated, this time, for a set copy, and placed it on the table. Turning to the intimidated waiting-lady, he said to her, in his highly-commanding tone:

"You will write this out as you see it. You will notice also that it is on the king's service!"

It happened that Lady Cosse prided herself on her handwriting. This vanity traveled side by side with his wish. She sat down, perking her head a little to one side like a flattered bird, and took up the pen critically. She began without trying to understand the text, for it is a tradition of letterers that comprehension is fatal to good work. In her antiquated hand, fine, cramped and small, she copied from the tall, sprawling, gigantic model, without exhibiting a shade of emotion. The betrayal of the league soon struck her as astonishing on the part of the leaguer-in-chief, but she did not really pause, up to the last period, save to renew the dip of ink.

He let her sprinkle the letter with golden sand, took it up, scanned it, nodded approval, as much at the faithfulness as at her refraining from comment, and, after folding it, corners in, put the last touch to it by affixing a drop of wax. She, only too eager to oblige, handed him the seal which belonged to her mistress, a chiseled chalcedone, in a silver handle.

He pressed on the yielding wax.

"If he does not know her hand, he must know her arms!" he jocularly said, but not aloud, for he did not expect the conceit to be relished or even comprehended.

He took out a purse, and laid it under the enlarged eyes of the perplexed woman.

"This, by a sure hand, by wish of your mistress," said he.

"That purse to the bearer?" inquired she, amazed at the generosity, even in a lover.

"No; that is for you!" said he, perhaps aware of her reputation for cupidity, as a worthy servant to Queen Catherine.

"Oh, that boy is the surest hand," said she, no doubt perceiving that such wages covered iniquity, and at once entering into the scheme, if there were one.

The duke thrust the key which he had in his pouch into the end of the missive.

Lady Cosse took both as they were, and went to the door, where Arthur, not daring to enter, was listening intently.

On seeing the address, his eyes were relieved of anxiety.

"Do you know his lodgings?" asked she.

"The Count of Megrin's?" repeated he, after reading. "Yes! rather twice than once! Mother, this will make the gentleman happy!"

"What did he say?" asked the duke, waiting impatiently till the door closed after the messenger's departure.

"That the letter would, he thought, make the receiver happy!"

"No doubt—it is intended for that end!" remarked the prince, enigmatically. "You are so, with that boon, too?"

"It is like your grace," said she, bowing as he went to the door.

He was between the princess and the only way out.

"Come he to her by any way," muttered he; "he must step over the stone which closes his sepulchre!"

He rejoined his men at the gateway with so light a step, spite of his battle array, and with so joyous a visage that the crowd cheered more heartily than before, and some said, enviously:

"He has been in there to visit his lady-love! He is to marry the Princess of Porcian as soon as he is approved chief of the Holy League!"

Within her room, bathing her bruises, which she would not fawn, nor, woman-like, permit

any eye to see, the princess heard the vocifera-
tions:

"Long live Henry of the League!"

This was a great prince! But love curled
her lip hatefully.

CHAPTER VIII.

FOLLOWING THE BAIT.

Arthur had made good speed to reach the palace of the Louvre. He found all there plunged into desolation, for the order countermanding the gala had overturned the joy of the servants and purveyors into misery.

He arrived at the council chamber without any satisfaction, but, luckily, a page of his acquaintance, with whom he had often fished for small fry along the river, pointed out the apartment assigned to St. Megrin.

"Make haste," said the other lad, "for the count has been made a duke, and if he defeats his antagonists in a mortal duel which is to come off immediately, he will not content himself with those dull rooms."

In the ante-chamber he was challenged by a German valet, who had accompanied his master since the German tour.

As the boy would not reveal more than that he was bearer of a confidential communication from a lady, he was compelled to show him into the count's own sitting-room.

The latter had no sooner seen the arms on the letter in the wax, than he dismissed his man and said, as he put the key on his finger and swung it there:

"Where do you come from?"

"If your lordship does not expect any letter, still you might have hoped for one."

"That may be, but——" He hesitated to open it. "Who are you, little Mercury?"

"A lord cannot be so ignorant of blazonry as to miss reading that emblem aright!" replied Arthur, pertly.

"It is true—I have seen this in Germany! Is it the princess——"

"You are about right," replied the page, laying his finger on his cherry lip.

"Did your mistress write this—did she send you with it to me?"

"Look at the address, if you will not believe your instinct about the contents."

"Did her hand give you this?"

"Well, do not kiss it, on the chance of error. I had it from an old and wrinkled one, direct!"

"Hem! Her confidante?"

"I guess so, for she is so old, decrepit and bungling that I doubt any one would employ her in a busy capacity."

"I do not know the handwriting, it is true!" said he; "but, then, I am newly come to court. If the go-between is her confidante——"

"Not so much so as I, being her kin, and of her choosing, whereas Lady Cosse is of the old queen's."

"Lady Cosse!"

"The mouse is out!" said Arthur. "I shall be flogged for this! and I am not accounted a babbler!"

"Where did you last see your lady?"

"Oh, she was dressing for the ball, and too trembling, pale and disturbed to be very eager about the new attire, which even I call remarkable!"

"Not care about a ball dress? This is likely! This concurs," said the count, allaying his apprehensions.

This might happen so, after the interview at the sorcerer's, and yet he had been far from expecting a love-note.

"Perhaps! See the lines!" suggested Arthur, thinking that the gallant was very timorous.

St. Megrin opened the epistle, and was amazed at its tenor, being so opposite to what he expected. Nevertheless, nothing could be a stronger proof of the writer's endeavor to spite a certain somebody, and so please her own friend, positively his foe, than to introduce a spy, friendly to the king intrigued against and betrayed, into the midst of the hostile cabal.

To elevate a champion, and defeat her loathed tyrant was characteristic of the more active women of the age.

Harbored by Catherine de Medici, this was work worthy of her instigation.

Still, fewer words, but breathing love rather than revenge, would have delighted him more.

Here was no illusion such as love-nonsense might have generated; paper, lines, key, counsel —all were very real.

To bring to the king in the morning indubitable evidence that Henry of Guise was marshaling his forces to dethrone his liege would be to hurl him down lower than if he smote him in the authorized combat of two!

The lover lost, but the royal favorite gained.

There was plain sense—to destroy her tyrant, and for him to confirm his new title was a stroke of policy worthy of the Queen of Navarre, arch-compound of the lady of beauty and statecraft.

"I am loved!" said he. "And worshiped!"

"May I say: 'Silence!' my lord?" said Arthur, a little frightened at the prospects he imagined, with full memory of how diabolical the

Duke of Guise had looked at him when he braved him.

"You are right, young sir! and you must be mute as the grave likewise! Forget what you have carried; what you have seen me receive, oh, so gladly! Forget my name! Forget your mistress', as well! She showed little prudence in charging you with this heavy burden, unless she knows you are prudent above your young years!"

"I think I can hold my peace! The still pig gets the draff! I heard that over the Rhine!"

"After all, they would not suspect a little elf like you of conveying weighty secrets!"

"Unless my pride in being the courier betray me!" said the boy with the blushing cheek.

"Hush! It is a grievous secret—one which enfolds the messengers like the two at the ends of his journey! Your eyes must not let out, your face must not reveal! You are young— keep the recklessness and gayety of your time!

If we meet again, pass me without a bow, or sign, or glance! There are thought-readers in the palace, who can gather whole volumes from little indications like that! In the future, if you should have similar correspondence to transmit, beg it not to be confided to perfidious paper, which is all men's informant! I will understand your look, your token, gesture! I can give you my purse, and refill it each time you send it to me empty—but——"

"Master, I am not wholly noble by birth, but the half of me which, they say, is so, would cleave apart that other part of me called 'mean' if it accepted pay for love's service. Some would not comprehend a talking marmoset like me, but I will not take your coin!"

"Take my hand, little noble! Some of these days, if we are on a battlefield together, and you bear yourself as you hold out the pennon to indicate—I trust to make you a knight!"

"I wish I were ten years older, and this the battlefield!" exclaimed Arthur.

"Faith, it may be as perilous! Mark, if ever you have need of me, and I survive the morrow, come to me and ask! You shall have all you crave, unto my heart's blood! Go out now —by the back stairs, and let no person see you or know you were with me. God have you and your mistress ever in His holy keeping!"

Arthur gave him a manly shake of the hand, and flitted away, with a knowing wink to imply that this was not the first time he had gone out of the palace surreptitiously.

St. Megrin was not allowed to doubt, on sober consideration, that this odd missive was at bottom one of love. A princess does not put all that she should hold dear in a chevalier's power without seeing its reach.

"I shall demolish all this fool's castle the duke is building, from which to assail my master! I shall in one night repay Henry for making me his champion!"

The clock in the courtyard, although erratic, struck ten. If he meant to carry out the daring route proposed it was necessary not to lose time.   He had to procure the costume of a citizen or one of the disbanded soldiers who enlisted in the league.

He was going to call for his valet when his path was blocked by a gloomy figure to be encountered in the court precincts. It was a monk of that order called the Saccophori, that is, wearers of sackcloth. He expected some such envoy from the king after the injunction from him to prepare religiously for his duel. But at this moment, with his heart beating high and his whole body buoyant, he did not thank this token of care for his spiritual safety. He was going to repulse the unwelcome adviser, when the hood fell back on the shoulders.

"Why, we have Master Ruggieri here!" exclaimed he, glad that this seeker after more than earthly knowledge could not have seen the page.

"I come from the queen-mother; she is anxious to know, if possible, the outcome of your approaching encounter with the Duke of Guise."

"No doubt!" impatiently. "I ought to be more eager—but I am filled with confidence! I am inspired with faith that I shall be the palm-bearer in this strife!"

"The palmbearer? That is, the martyr—the defeated here, to triumph above?"

"No! no! My ideas are wholly worldly. My master, I am pitted against a hypocrite and traitor. I, the loyal servitor, must win, or where would be the justice of Heaven? Not on this globe!"

"Here, sometimes!"

"Well, what do you see on my hand?"

"Bloodshed—profuse, malignant, mortal."

"Very possible! On my brow? I can answer that; nothing but happiness—look you! I love and I am beloved."

He had forgot who had shown him the object of this incredible passion when he thus spoke enthusiastically.

"On your brow—reflection of the starlight!"

The groom of the chambers had not brought in lights. The gleam of the stars, crossing over the grotesque ornamentation of the old walls, slightly illumined the young man's gleaming features.

"There is death impending!" said the Italian, solemnly.

"Yes, it will be a conflict to the death."

"Remember Captain DuGuast, my son!" said the astrologer. "He mocked at the warning from the stars! and he——"

"They butchered him on the sick bed—his friends have told me the story—butchers who did not dare look askew at him in the broad day and on the broad street! Now, I—I never felt better and stronger and clearer-headed in all my life! The man at the point of my blade dies, unless an angel intervenes, and I should thrust at the angel, believing it must be false, that undertook to save the perfidious Duke of Guise!"

"Well, if this time to-morrow you can look at me with those undimmed eyes, then I swear that you will count many long and happy days! Do you see those two stars?"

"I see multitudes of stars—enough in which to people all the Christians of this earth!"

"But those two, there, of a ruddy light, in the Chambers of the South! They are yours and your chief 'distanctor!' They are going to come into conjunction—and but one will emerge free and triumphant."

"The other——"

"Will have plunged forever into the dark!"

"The dark? What is that, doctor?"

Ruggieri looked at him so close that their brows almost touched.

"If I knew that, my son, I should be lord of this palace—lord over all the palaces in the world! Now, farewell and fight well! I am always in the dark."

St. Megrin let him go. He was left in mood-

"Ruggieri looked at him so closely that their brows almost touched."
See page 134.

iness, unbearable after he had been blissful; although he did not wholly believe now in the visionary's prophecies, he could not recover the former state of ecstasy.

He shrank from this reference to DuGuast, whose murder was attributed to the Duke of Guise, whether impelled in the first instance by Queen Marguerite or not. This hint that the duke, scorning to meet, even on the footing which the king had made equal, the count, not comparable with a tried warrior and sovereign prince, thought it no despicable act to employ assassins, was sufficient to make a hothead revolve the future a little. And St. Megrin was not a madcap like the other minions.

"At least," sighed he, "if, like him, I am to be set upon by the whole pack of hangman's dogs, let it be after I shall have heard my beloved say that she loves me and me alone!"

In this partly-regained pleasure, he was visited by Joyeuse, whom the valet preceded, bearing a candelabrum lighted in its three or four branches.

Joyeuse was radiant as the flambeau.

"Oh, have you been shriven?" said he. "I stumbled upon a friar at the door! Or did he come from Friend Harry to bless Schomberg's sword and take away the bad luck which let it defend him ill?"

One could not be angry with this moth.

"No, it was not a man holy, except by his garb! He is a reader of the stars."

"Oh, a rival of old Ruggieri? It is time we had a fortune-teller who would tell one's fate without bad French! With what has the new consulter of the spangles on the eternal robe had to cheer you?"

"Nothing. I was looking to read my own version there."

"I would rather look down—and follow not their flight, but that of a marvelously-pretty urchin whom I passed in the yard. Faith! for plumpness and bloom of cheek it might have been young Lady Charolais in boy's trunks and long-nosed shoes; or, at least, the cousin of a lady who sends him out on her love errands."

"Joyeuse," continued the count, trying to direct his gaze upward out of the window, "do you believe that, after our quittance with earthly friends, we mount aloft by those ladders of luster to a dizzy plane to meet friends gone before?"

"What thoughts! They have never come to me! The stars on the beaker's brim—the bubbles of mirth on Lesbian lips, the sparkle of those stars of the mint—these delight and enthrall me. Why, would you have me deny my name, my device? What! would our slogan be '*Hilariter! be jolly!*' if I moped and hung on the glinting of stars so far out of reach? Be joyful does for this world; to eat heartily, share with friends, laugh with sinners, whose laugh is so musical! As for any other world than that

the Spanish have discovered, a fig! only, I hope
the people there have no tailors' bills to foot
and no tight boots, like these in fashion, to pay
for, when their rents come to town!"

St. Megrin, turned from him with pain at the
jar. He went on musing without seeing him.

"No doubt we are joined there to those from
whom we were reft here!"

"Apropos, if you precede me—and, without
damping your ardor, Guise is in trim to stick
some one through for that snub before the king
—let Quelus know that I settled with the host
of the Horn of Plenty, and paid for ten masses
at St. Genevieve's."

"Do you believe that eternity is but another
name for bliss?"

"In some case it will be for blistering. That
is for your opponent. If you do not cut short
his career, he will, through pride, extend his list
of atrocities beyond Lucifer's! But you must
be going out of your everyday wits! What

deuced language is this? You will sicken even
the king, who holds forth not so badly in such
humdrum morality. Or, if you must be mad,
be so wholly, so that you will walk over the
body of Lorraine like Orlando Furioso over a
wind-thrown oak in the forest!"

"You talk best! I must not be mad."

"Come to my rooms—I have received some
Rhenish wine which the carrier misdescribed as
'Neckar'; the ignorant ass should have written
'Nectar!' It is too good for that sour-faced
Epernon. But haste, for Bussy was dipping his
mustache in it; and drop your mien of a
Huguenot who hears a drinking song. One
will be saying that you are not afraid of a slash
or stab, but sorry you have a quarrel so desira-
ble on hand!"

"Sorry?" repeated the other, firing up. "I
throw all off my shoulders! If I should be
killed, I must carry away the consolation that
he left his life under my corpse!"

"If I were a sexton, at that, I would run and toll the bell for Guise.   I consider him dead."

He thrust his arm into the loop of his friend's and bore him off in his communicative "hilarity."

CHAPTER IX.

IN SMOOTH WATERS.

When Joyeuse and his ward arrived at the former's suite, they were confounded by finding the place empty; but they were consoled that the same vacancy did not exist in the German wine bottles. But they were given no time to finish what Bussy had left—in his desire to be pot-valiant in meeting the king—by the servant hastening to say that he had been called away by a page. This messenger, direct from the royal master, had added that he was summoning to the second throneroom all the courtiers, by which they were included.

They were almost the last to arrive. The king was established in one of his pre-assemblages, when he was at ease and discussed matters with his favorites as an old host with his cronies. But this time the reminiscence of his previous cohort being defeated by the

Guisard party deepened his foreboding about the present series.

"Be at ease!" said he, loudly, to still his own fever—"be quite at ease, for our measures are taken. I called for you, Lord Bussy, to restore our friendship because of your valorous seconding of our brave St. Megrin."

Bussy bowed to the new duke, and then to the king.

"Why did you not come to see me sooner?" asked Henry of the favorite. "Gentlemen, my mother is to form part of this council. Let her be notified that we are present."

A page had placed a stool of honor on the first elevation of the dais. All stared to see if this favor was destined for Bussy or the new-made peer. It was for St. Megrin, into whose ear, at this convenient place, the monarch wished to whisper.

The queen-mother had come in. There was a rumor coming before that the Duke of Guise was in the anteroom.

St. Megrim, at this, assumed a frown which tallied badly with the signal honor done him, and which Catherine perceived with inward disapproval.

Epernon, who had assumed much gravity since the astrologer had promised him elevation, took the place of the absent secretary.

Catherine bent forward to converse quietly with her son, but this was impossible with St. Megrin's head between.

"Be easy, mother," said Henry, as if he had not raised this barrier; "I have given my word to conduct this affair like a patriarch of gravity and moderation. I have prayed—and 'God's blessing gained, all else attained.'"

He delighted in these scraps of a profane "Logia," picked up in saturnalia, rather than ecclesiastical penetralia.

In the same martial accoutrements in which he had appeared backed by the League, but without the city magnates, the Duke of Guise returned to his theme.

With what might pass for modesty, neither he nor his antagonist looked fixedly at each other, but it was intensity of hate. In one sentiment they met—each wished this matter, though so important, to be removed from the way of the private stroke they contemplated.

Besides, the king, of whom one was never sure, claimed all the ambitious general's attention. It was a conflict of cobra and ichneumon —a side glance, and all was lost with the inadvertent one.

But it was in a pleasant, acquiescent voice that the royal Henry spoke:

"We had the first thought to draw up the act arranged about, but we recalled that a somewhat similar deed was couched by the clerks and lawyers for Lord Humieres, what time he induced the nobility of Peronne and Picardy to put their signatures to it. It could not be better. As for the nomination of the chief, an article at the foot will cover all amply, and no doubt you may have some suggestions to make about that?"

Certainly, Guise was ready with suggestions, or, more plainly, he had so thoroughly thought it over that he had spared the king all worry about it.

Henry thanked him still effusively for the kindness, and, as the prince drew out of his pages' budget a writing, he nodded for Epernon to take it.

The baron proceeded to read it aloud, with a full voice, to the effect:

Association made between the Princes, Nobles, Gentry and others concerned, as well for the ecclesiastics as the noble, of the Land of Picardy. In the first place——

"Pray wait, Epernon," interrupted the king. "We know this statement well, for we have had the duplicate. It is useless to read the twenty——"

"Eighteen, to be exact, majesty——"

"Over-numerous articles which compose it. Go straight to the end. And if you will but draw nearer, duke, you can dictate what you wish. Reflect what it means to name the head for so mighty a congregation! Such a chief will wield great powers."

Guise's face flushed with expectant joy.

"Cousin, dear, in a word, act as for yourself."

This was at the same time plain as pretty speaking, as Joyeuse whispered to Halde.

Henry of Lorraine ought to have suspected from the too-agreeable progress and the old queen's ominous silence under her set smile, like an experienced actress', that his captured trust was beyond recall. He assured the king that he would be content with the outcome.

The statesmen looked hard at the monarch, whose genial serenity disturbed them more than a frown or a scowl. But there was no opening for an interference.

Guise was thoughtfully forming his phrases in his mind, and as Epernon, taking a fresh dip of ink on the crow quill, glanced up for the commencement, he dictated, with slowness and due emphasis, as follows, the king nodding at every pause like a musician beating time to an appreciated air:

Primo: The person honored by His Majesty's choice should be issue of a sovereign house, worthy of the affection and the trust of the French by his past conduct and his faith in the established religion.

The churchmen bowed, and Henry rattled his rosary approvingly.

Secundo: The title of Lord Lieutenant of the Kingdom will be conferred upon him, and the troops will be set under his commands.

He looked at the military men, and they preserved a perfect silence, yet they acknowledged the speaker's warlike worth. The king, as if this was not in his province, simply assented by silence.

Tertio: As his actions will only aim at the betterance of the sainted cause, he will have none to render account to but Heaven and his own conscience.

The silence was weightier than before, but as the royal critic only hemmed and said: "That will do," all breathed freely.

St. Megrin had been fidgeting on his stool.

At this he ventured to bring his lips to the king's ear and murmur:

"Did you say: 'Well?' Can your highness approve such conditions so that a man will be arrayed with such powers?"

"Let it pass," in the same tone.

"But this will smother your realm with war and blood."

"Tut, tut, not this chief! Enough, there— be still. We wish, be it understood—we desire positively that the choice should be convenable to you whatever it be. Therefore, as a good and loyal subject, cousin, set us an example of submission. After me you are the foremost in the realm."

This was ignoring the Duke of Anjou, and the remark made the queen lose her smile.

"In this case, too, you are interested in my being obeyed."

This was sailing in such smooth waters that Guise did not presume to ruffle it with the least objection. In fact, he had never used a more suave and unctuous accent as he replied, with frankness like a blunt soldier:

"Sire, I acknowledge in advance, as chief of the holy union, whomsoever your majesty designates, and I shall regard as a rebel"—he raised his voice sonorously—"any one who braves his orders."

"This is handsome, my lord duke," said the king, slyly stroking his own hands, as if smoothing on a glove. "Write, Epernon."

He stood upon the throne, apart from his chair, with much grandeur, self-possession and inward satisfaction at having angled, secured his fish and brought it under the gaff.

"Write: 'We, Henry of Valois, by the grace of God King of France and Poland, approve, by the present act drawn up by our faithful and beloved cousin, Henry of Lorraine, Duke of Guise, the association known as the Holy League, and by our authority, declare as the chief—our noble selves!'"

Guise gripped his dagger hilt, as habitual with

him at being crossed, and faltered through his clinched teeth:

"How now?"

A subdued ironical laughter made the circuit, and Joyeuse, who would have laughed in Satan's beard, chuckled audibly.

Henry lifted his hand, commandingly, nay, imperiously, for none to interrupt him, and went on, with his voice quite strong with self-sufficiency:

"In token of which, we affix our royal seal!"

Stepping off the lowest step, and cunningly nudging St. Megrin with his knee, in passing him, he took the pen from his secretary *pro tem*, continuing:

"And we sign with our own hand!"

With probably the firmest strokes his vacillating hand had ever traced a line, he wrote a large:

"HENRY OF VALOIS!"

Guise seemed to have his eyes seared by this line, where he had expected, without any doubt, to have seen "Guise" in lieu of "Valois." He shrank from the pen which the other tendered to him with a very steady hand.

"Your turn," said the king, with much cunning, taking great care not to let the least irony filter into his tone, "for are you not the next comer, first after us?"

He appeared astonished at the continued hesitation.

"Do you think that the name of the Valois and our flower-of-the-lily do not figure as worthily at the base of this deed as the name of Henry of Guise and the Lorraine blackbirds? By the fame of our race! you only asked for the name of the man most endeared to the French!" He smiled superciliously and with infatuation. "Are we not so beloved?" looking around to receive the flattering murmur.

"Who loves, teases!" said Catherine, to her neighbors.

"Reply according to your heart," resumed the sovereign. "You sought a gentleman of the highest nobility! I believe I am as good a gentleman as any! Sign, my lord, sign! for it is you said it: He who would not assent to this must be a rebel!"

The duke looked straight at the queen, and it was clear that some understanding had once existed between her and the Lorraines, for, clearly, he now reproached her. The king did not seem to perceive this, for he had let his eyes fall on the paper, pointing out the blank. He indicated the place under his angular, sprawling sign-manual.

The weak king's favorites had none of them looked for this strong hand. Joyeuse irreverently stood up beside Guise, and as irreverently said, like a fellow to another at signing as witness a vulgar marriage contract, "After you, my lord!"

A little more and he would have jogged his elbow.

"Yes, gentlemen, let us all be upon this testimonial to union!" pursued the king, merrily and with heartiness, more like his brother-king of Navarre. "Epernon, see to it that copies of this excellent agreement are distributed throughout the realm!"

The temporary secretary could not speak for suppressed mirth at the duke's dismay. He nodded several times, like a toy mandarin.

Antraguet made bold to whisper to his lord: "Write with their ink until you can write in their blood! Bah! first shot miss—the next tells home!"

The duke lifted his somewhat fallen crest. He shook his helmet so that the feathers seemed to curl up against a passing blight.

He sullenly set his name, passed the pen to the eager hand of Joyeuse, and withdrew as soon as etiquette permitted it.

A court official at the door whispered to Antraguet, who, in turn, said, covertly, to his master:

"The Duke of Mayenne is in town!"

"Ah, you will take orders from him!" returned the commander.

Henry was apologizing to the nobles for the long session, at which, more than the others, St. Megrin had chafed. "It is decidedly dull as compared with a masked ball, but lay all the blame of it on the shoulders of our cousin of Guise! He forced me into it! Fare thee well, duke of my bosom—lord of my heart!" he called out. "Cease not to look after the state interests, like the good and leal subject you show yourself! And never forget that whomsoever obeyeth not the chief whom we appointed will be declared guilty of high treason! Upon which, I abandon ye to the keeping of God on high! All may go!"

He made a gesture for St. Megrin to remain. He went to his mother, as the pages took her train, and added, quietly:

"Did I carry it off nicely?"

"Yes, son; but do not forget that I——"

"No, no, or, should I do so, you will please jog my mind!"

The courtiers followed out the duke, and abstained from any whispering which might add petty nips to the severe pinch under which his breast was turning black.

St. Megrin had obeyed the royal hint with irritation. He was ordered to linger, and his lady-love had set him a mission of consequence. He was like one of those mariners who wish to speed with the tide, but some siren under the wave strives to detain, to divert and bear him away in another direction.

On being surely alone, Henry let his laugh find vent without any restraint. Few had heard him thus frank in his real feeling.

CHAPTER X.

FORWARD TO LOVE AND DEATH.

"Well, my bosom Saint! have I not fully profited by your friendly counsel?" said he. "I have dethroned the king of Paris and the old creed, and behold me, **chief of the** Leaguers in his stead!"

"May you never repent it, sire! but this idea did not come from this quarter, or of your own impulse——"

"No! It is from—oh, you may cite the mother-wit of our family!"

"Yes, I recognize her wily policy!"

"You are not widely out, sir—for, in faith," said the hypocrite, "I am all sincerity and straightforwardness by myself. She believes that she gains everything when she gains time. I suspect that she has a club up her sleeve for the Duke of Guise. I heard her call him, in her sweetest voice. 'her friend!' That was ominous!   I saw that you put your hand to the document with regret!"

"I? Not at all! Rather, you hesitated, almost like the duke!"

"Yet you were monarch—now you are but chief of a party!"

"Henry of Navarre would give his left hand to be in my place. What else was to be done?"

"Cast aside all this policy out of the Florentine merchants' books, and act openly!"

"In what manner—be precise—be open yourself!"

"Like a king! that is A-B-C! If you lack proofs of the under-play of this plotting lord, I will furnish them—and before twenty-four hours pass!"

"If I have them, I, as pilot of the ship of state, will punish all for the mutiny!"

"With them in hand, you would try and judge him?"

"I should have to do so with a royally-appointed tribunal, for the Parliament is all for

him.   They would not do him the unkindness
to hale him before their bar!"

"Then on the Parliament impose the power
of your will!   The Bastile has strong walls,
deep and wide moats, and a faithful governor.
Put Lord Guise inside it, and let him be
brought out to the execution-yard, in the steps
of Marshals Montmorency and Cosse!"

"Tut, tut, no walls are stout enough, no
ditches deep enough, to keep in such a prisoner!"

"Who follow the raven must come to ruin!"

"Ruins of the Bastile, perhaps—all Paris is
a great mass—they could fill up the moats and
pile up under the ramparts so that one could
step off upon the battlements!"

"There are too many Henrys at a time!"
persisted St. Megrin.

"My young friend, I do not know anything
that would weigh down that restless frame but
a wrapper of lead and a press-board of granite!
It is for you, since you are bound by your

challenge, to make him fit and ripe for shroud and bier! I then charge myself with the rolling out of the leaden sheet and the building of the stone coffin!"

"If I kill him as a gentleman should, he will be punished, but not as he merits!"

"Pish! little matters the inadequacy of your means, as long as the result is the same!" said the Valois, carelessly. For this little display of energy had exhausted his scant stock of virility. "Talking of your combat, I hope that you have neglected nothing in the way of meet preparations?"

"Well, no, sire, for the material, but," with some halting, for he knew that his master was a stickler for pious precautions at times, "I have been engrossed in thoughts which preclude religious duties, although they turn on the utmost virtue and grace."

"You have not found time for that?" said Henry, in a doleful voice. "Have you not learned, by my example, to resist mundane pleasures, and crown your life?"

"So short a time under your model," stammered the courtier.

"It is true—you were not here to witness the duel of Jarnac and Chataignerie! What a loss!   It was fierce, and all went awry because both did not attend prayers!"

"I thought that one dealt the other a foul stroke!" objected the count.

"Let me tell you! The battle was set for a fortnight after the defiance. Jarnac passed the time in prayers, while Chataignerie spent the time in futile pastimes, without thinking that the angels do nothing more than play the *viol de gamba* and the violin, as in Fra Angelico's paintings, of which I am promised two masterpieces, by the Holy Father, by the by! Well, he was punished out of the skies, my poor, inattentive St. Megrin!"

"Why, I thought, as all say, that Jarnac the pious cut him below the belt—that is to say, hamstrung him, as a clodpoll does a steed with his hedge-knife! It was not a thunderbolt—Jove's eagle would have been ashamed of such a blow of his beak in that quarter!"

"At all events, Jarnac very properly paid for candles to his saint, in perpetuity!"

"Sire, at least, I am contrite!"

"I fear that, contrition being a virtue, is all the virtue you will die with, at this rate!"

"I try to do my duty to my king, my love and my saint! But the first I placed, is the first to appeal to me, to command me—I must confuse your enemies, sire!"

"What! set me foremost?" said the king, weakening and protesting, in false modesty.

"Sire, I am but an instrument in the holy hands—now, if I have been chosen to be the battering-beam to procure the downfall of your greatest opponent, Heaven's will be done!"

"That sounds very pretty and falls soft on my ear, but what are you talking about, my lord? Your existence since I made you prince of the court belongs to the State!"

"My lord, I thought that I had the honor to assert that I hope this night, almost this hour, to wrest from traitorous hands the secrets which will overturn the Duke of Guise! More to be dreaded than Henry of Navarre is—that hero of the unveiled tented field! I must repay the rank and other boons I owe to my king and my master in the best way offered me!"

"You are speaking aptly. To be sure, if you were acting on your own business, you ought not to get rashly killed off-hand! And the more, if you are acting for the State, we must beseech you to take every care to be successful without loss of life! A useful man must be often useful. What would be the good of changing a sword because it once served well?"

"I have more than one reason for selling my skin dearly; believe that, sire!"

"I doubt not that you will do your best. I

wish that you and Bussy would cross swords a little time for practice!"

"I must attend to my devotions, if I get a moment," said St. Megrin, with the royal whine.

"You jackanapes!" pinching him by the ear. "To do your best is not enough against a camp terror like that Guise! We will make him take oath at the altar not to be shielded by secret mail, talisman or charms. That rogue Ruggieri has had a visit of his lately, and it was to deal in deviltry, I'll be bound! When we get him thus disarmed, gather up all your nerves, sinews, and courage and, ha! push at him!" He imitated the thrust of a sword, with his arm extended and his hand flat, and added, with a ghastly smile:

"Be expeditious, for his death is expedient."

St. Megrin bowed his head.

"He is in the way of many, my lord!"

"Once delivered of that stumbling block, do

you see, count, there will no longer be two
Lords of Paris! I shall be veritably the ruler!"

"In and about Paris," said the favorite; "but
as for the country——"

"Oh, Henry, the Captain? I will make him
my captain-general, and he will be content.
Henry is not a grasping, greedy plotter! He
hates and he loves aboveboard! Oh, we
would be good brothers if that brother Francis
of mine had not come between!"

"He is thrust between!" ventured the other.

"Oh, the queen-mother? It is true—she
adores that scapegrace of the Valois! But
she will esteem me now because I disembarrass
her of these Lorraines! And so she will like
you for actually plying the broom which
sweeps the palace clear of them and their webs!
That advice to counter on him did emanate
from her, and she will do anything for me on
account of this my obedience!"

"Sire, I am happy; you may tell her majesty

that my sword can be of service at the same time to her."

"That is pertinent. We will try that sword of yours, and your arm."

He rang a bell suspended by a cord from the wall.

A servant instantly opened a door.

"Call Lord Halde," said Henry, "and let several pair of sound foils be brought with him."

"Foils," repeated the favorite, "at this hour, when your majesty has need of repose?"

"Repose! Repose! Do you din me with that owl's cry? Repose! Do you believe that I get any sleep between Guise hammering up recruits at every door in Paris and Henry of Navarre singing psalms of deliverance at every cottage door in the South! I wager that neither of them do much slumbering! Or if they doze, they dream! Shall I tell you of what those two Henrys dream? Of snatching the crown off my head, on which it is riveted, I believe, by the pangs its thorns give me! Sleep!

They themselves see that I can rest nowhere unless it is in a monastery! I like the quiet of the monastery, but my doctor has assured me that monotony would be my death, and I am only fickle, frivolous, and irregular in my attendance at chapel because I require variety! A king gets no sleep, my brand-new duke, and the born dukes will tell you the same. Is Halde never coming with those irons?"

St. Megrin imitated the king by pacing the room with enfevered steps. He thought of the clandestine session, and that, perhaps, the writer of the denunciation was even now waiting at the door of which he had the key to let him in. He stamped his foot, stopped, and clapping his hand to his head, said, impatiently:

"Sire, you recall me to my duty. I see that I must go to the midnight mass at St. Sulpice's. My preparations should be accomplished in that holy fane."

"Never mind the fencing lesson, then, but it is a pity."

The door opened, but Halde was turned to stone on the threshold by an imperative gesture, and had to retire, with his page carrying a sheaf of fencing tools, like a bird of Jupiter with his electric arrows.

"Hark!"

The innumerable bells of Paris were, with more or less concord, repeating the stroke of twelve.

"It is midnight."

"Alas! if all is not too late, it is midnight!" sighed St. Megrin.

"I will myself go and pray."

"All need it—I, not least of all your true servants."

"As far as the holy chrism sanctifies me, I bless you, my son," and Henry spoke kindly, if not paternally. "We must part, but you shall come to me on the morrow. I have a marsh-pike, a *pogge* out of the St. Germain ponds, stuffed with breadcrumbs and chopped leeks, which—— But since Halde had swords, if he escorts you, eh?"

"I must execute my mission alone."

"Mission?"

"I mean go to the place of communion alone."

"I rely on you everywhere. You have not been spoilt by the lures of the town. You are not entangled by a Delilah. Act for the fear of God and the glory of the king."

"For your weal, my lord. I am glad that I satisfy my king."

"Yes, the king is so, and your friend must be so. Here." He drew the knight toward him and, glancing about furtively to be sure no one perceived that he would fortify his champion as he sought to prohibit the adversary from being protected, he went on, throwing over his neck a gold chain, with a small box at the end. "This is a fragment of the true cross, direct from Rome. Joyeuse brought it, and I do not think he would, if he had lost it, have substituted a piece of willow cut at the wayside for it.   Oh, that has been done!   Well, Pope Gregory assures me that the wearer cannot die of fire, iron or the pest.   You can return it to me after you defeat the enemy."

"If it is so potent, I would not deprive you for a moment."

"I?   Oh, I am not in danger.   It is only despots that are threatened."

"Oh, you are an overkind master," said the count, sincerely.

"Hold it; there may be an honest friend, even under the royal mantle."

He gave him the embrace as to a knight about starting on his most dangerous deed of daring.

"Wait," said he, "and I will send you a parting cup of Alicante wine."

St. Megrin did not intend to wait for this nonessential favor.   He hurried to his rooms, where his man had a dress ready, under which he might traverse the dark and unsafe streets.

"Haste, George, haste," he kept saying.

"If you are going out, shall I send for a porter's chair?"

"No; I must make short cuts to reach my destination swiftly.   Oh, I have lost so much time."

"The streets will be fraught with footpads!"

"Not at all.   It looks squally; those unwashed dogs will not face old Januarius, who might clean them with a dash from his urn."

"If you have a good horse.   I know the groom of the stables."

"A horse?   I must leap all the street chains, then!   No, I go afoot!"

He looped up his boot tops with the thong provided for the purpose, and tied them securely.

"If I go along, with a good arquebuse from the guardroom?"

"The rain will put out the match."

"I can carry a cutlass!"

"Your anxiety is out of place!   I have a dagger along with my fighting sword, which was poor Schomberg's!   It is strong and heavy."

George had gone to look out of the window.

"Strange," said he; "you may not be without fellow foot passengers.   Look! doors open covertly; shadows issue and flit along as if going to the Witches' Sabbath."   He signed himself over the breast with his crossed fingers.

"Oh, ho! it is a meeting of good citizens who run to congratulate the Duke of Guise on being made lieutenant of the League!"

"Oh, if that is all!"

"Stay!"   He drew the servant's knife-of-all-work from his girdle and cut off his right love-lock.   He tied it with a piece of his cuff ribbon and said, as he laid this on the table:

"If I return no more, give this to a little rosy-cheeked page who came here this day, and is, I think, sure to return for news of me, if I am not home in a few days.   Where is my dun cloak?"

George wrapped him up and left play for drawing the sword.

"I am sorry you must go out, my dear young master! There will be sad grief at St. Megrin if you are not seen there with a bride, as all believe you should bear thither out of this accursed den of thieves.   The night will be terrible!"

Indeed, black clouds were heaping up over Montmarte, and a shed of lightning now and then showed how thick it was.

"Do not hang on to my cloak.   I am late as it is—perhaps, all too late——"

"Oh, if I might follow you!"

"Stay! Look to your own nose, sirrah!"

"My master, those shadows are highwaymen! They will peel you white and take doublet and hose!"

"Bah! when one steers for the mark I have in sight," said the gallant at the door, still repulsing him, "weather is nothing—the good prow beats through!"

"Woe!" moaned the faithful servant. "But the young will rub the velvet off their horns! They will——"

"Up!   Do not make a praying desk of a joint

stool!" cried a merry voice, as Joyeuse, at the head of a trail of other gallants, bounded into the room. "Halloa! ho! where is your invisible prince?"

George explained that the count had gone forth alone, and "as fast as if for thieving."

"What a miss!" cried Bussy, who was of the throng; "I counted on him!"

"What is it now?" asked Halde, who came up breathless from having been detained on the king's errand, frustrated, as we know.

"Why, the sounding of midnight seemed a signal. The burghers are pouring out to offer their condolements, for all I know, to their snubbed leader! Henry so cleverly supplanted him! Antraguet slipped out in his track, muttering that we should repay for our deriding him and his master! Boys, I foresee that there may be fun in disturbing their wailing. Who is with me for a prowl?"

"I," said St. Luc. "I am not going to let my

brother saint, Megrin, have all the fun of the street brawls to himself!"

"Muster the servants! Arm! arm!"

"And," said the prudent Epernon, rubbing the ink off his finger ends from his unaccustomed clerical labors, "not so much noise! Tell the king's gentleman-of-the-night that we are gone to the midnight mass at St. Over-the-hills!"

Silently, therefore, as those vague forms which St. Megrin and his valet had seen pass in the streets, this party glided out of the wicket of the river gate and betook themselves on the traces of their friend.

CHAPTER XI.

THE DECOY DOVE.

It was very well for the king's favorites—in the night gloom and from a high window—to take for good citizens, though of warlike habits, those who walked the streets around the place at midnight.

St. Megrin, descended to the level, could judge them more accurately.

They were not even the gutter-searchers and gypsies who lurked for remnants, but men gathering like vultures for one intention, and that a feast to the liking of birds of carnage.

They were badly dressed, but their clothing was military after the miscellaneous fashion when each raiser of a regiment clothed his companies as best his credit among drapers and accoutrement-makers permitted. Their coats were tattered and patched, their armor incomplete and past burnishing; but their weapons were in excellent order, as befitted what was not only to guard the owners' lives, but earn them a meal.

As for the lodgings, they did not sleep at night, and such pothouses as were their daily resort, furnished straw for debauches to be slept off upon.

For a while, the adventurer did not pay them any more heed than they gave him. For, in his sober attire, and carrying a long sword, they might, without any stretch of the imagination, assume he was of their kind.

But as he approached New Soissons House, he perceived some relations established between these men, apparently marching to a rendezvous and loungers at the corners, who kept aloof from the city watch and who exchanged watchword and answer with the passers.

"They are Guiseards, and there is a congress this night! As they are wending their way, with easy *pads*, like wolves, I conjecture that there is plenty of time."

Nevertheless, he did not view the prospect with equanimity, since these carriers openly of forbidden weapons, such as *mort-axes* (death-axes), partisans, bills, and even two-handed swords, promised that the spy discovered, amid a meeting, would be hacked to pieces, instead of being put in prison to abide an examination.

"Guise is kinging it already," thought he.

Prudently, therefore, he made the entire circuit of the block of buildings, very disconnected or coupled with irregular flying buttresses and arches, beams which might be withdrawn, and ropes which, used in peace times for the bleaching of linen, might, in war times, hang an enemy or lower a fugitive to the street.

A few lights sparkled in the upper part of the new mansion, where the servants were telling stories or playing cards with caution, as became the hour; it was shuttered and curtained almost hermetically elsewhere. As for the old building, except where a red fire glowed at a crevice or two and denoted that Ruggieri's furnace kept up the unflagging heat to cook "the philosopher's stone," it had the same obscurity and loneliness. The turn-again lane was black as the throat of one of those enormous dragons which artists represent as the entrance to the infernal regions.

Still shadows crossed one another in its depths, and the cavalier judged that they were keeping a kind of watch.

At one place only was there abnormal vivacity.

A corner of Old Soissons House, unconnected with that left off to the magician, as well it might be, since its employment was foreign to his grave and lofty studies, blazed at the bottom if gloomy at the top.

It was a little wineshop, dignified, after the hours when the taverns closed under the police regulations, by having the insatiable topers and homeless revelers swarm to it as the sole shelter in that ward.

It had no name, but a signpost, never adorned

with a signboard, bore a bush—in contradiction
to the old saying that "Good wine needs no
bush."

Good or bad, as regards its cellar, it had a
roaring fire—not to warm by, but to cook what
the customers, for the most part, brought under
their arms, as to a thieves' kitchen. It had
candles which a chandler would have pronounced cast for church uses. And the fireplace
was ample to accommodate the pieces of meat
and fowl which the vagrants watched cooking
and stood ready to guard if a rascal pretended
that he had confided the bone of contention to
the cook and his aid.

Into this drinking hole—it was little better—
the men whom St. Megrin had observed to follow his own path, dropped one by one, but only
to drink, whereupon, looking to their weapons
while in the vivid light, they stole out, pairing
off now and betaking themselves to pre-ar-
ranged resorts.

The lane sheltered them, no doubt, immediately after this refreshment.

Twice the count passed this busy meeting-place, and the second time he fancied that a man of superior costume was paying coin to the ruffians. This was done liberally, to judge by the grin on the faces, and he muttered:

"This does not seem to be natural enthusiasm for the League that he is kindling. Ah, grease the wheels well and one may travel far!"

As yet he could only suppose that a conventicle of the holy cause was to be attended by the men.

"It will be no fool's work to enter into their midst, if these be their outposts," thought he. "Luckily, I expect to have a pass, and I have the key—only, how find the door to suit this key?"

Again making the entire circuit, concluding that the tavern, the lane or even Ruggieri's hall would hardly be the seat of this convocation, he paused at the south side of the new mansion.

A capacious carriage gateway showed that

the architect, a foreseeing man, had planned for vehicles which would be wider than the hand or hose litter still fashionable, or rather compulsory by the narrowness of the old streets.

Here, in the fixed attitude of a fakir or a man of the time who was doing penance by inaction before a road cross, a figure in a cloak was standing, vaulted over by the arch. It was not tall and was so rounded that it occurred to him that it might be the page who had visited him in the Louvre.

But, on approaching with a warning cough, he found out his mistake. It was a woman.

An old woman, too, or wearing a gray wig, for he saw that the hair under a jeweled head-dress was lined with white.

This figure, man or woman, looked at him with intent eyes. He had no doubt that he was expected to speak, but he saw at the instant some one at the top of the street. He used the utmost caution, and, as the only token common to him and his mysterious correspondent—

whom as yet he could only surmise about—he held up the key accompanying the missive.

This seemed satisfactory, for the figure rapped ostentatiously at a little door shaped in the large double one. Then, as if her errand was done, she slipped away so smartly that he believed had he taken his eyes off her for a second he would have lost all trace.

He walked up to the door, reasoning that her soft knocking would be the signal for some one within to open it. It was an error. It had not moved; at a shake it did not budge. But he perceived a keyhole at the level of his breast, to which his key might fitly be applied.

Indeed, it fitted.

He thrust it in and looked around to see if his act was approved. But the mysterious figure had vanished, and in the stead stood two of those soldiers of "Lord Icannotell's corps."

Not wishing to be challenged now at the threshold of a possible inlet to the labyrinth, he turned the key, which acted like a charm, and pushed the panel open enough for him to slide through.

He closed it sharply, and, though it was bad policy thus to cut off communication with the outer world, he fastened it with a swing bar in the teeth of the two men. They marched past, without having noticed how he had disappeared, if they had been conscious of his presence.

He examined his refuge.

It ought to have been the yard, but the timbers and stones were lying about to finish the works. He was in a kind of workshop, and at the inner end was the wall of the main building, of fresh-cut yellow stone, out of the St. Denis quarries.

He found there that a door, temporarily constructed while a famous one in carved oak would replace it, was left ajar—no doubt, for his benefit.

There was no doubt; he was expected. The rest was left to his instinct if no other guide was furnished. He appreciated the delicacy of the betrayer, who did not care to be found in his company if he was discovered prematurely.

"It is in Soissons House that the meeting will be held," he pondered. "Very likely; the Countess of Montafix is kin to the Lorraines. It is odd, though, that at the same time as this denunciation is confided to me, the Princess of Porcian should be under the same rooftree!"

This name on his lips inspired him to more venturesomeness.

He opened the door and passed through it. As he closed it, he heard at the wineshop this precious contribution to the ballads of the day —quite a different vein to his friend, Ronsard's:

> "The spry hand, the sly hand—
> That's my hand in thy hand!
> Can win o'er the high hand,
> On ocean or dry land!
> *Noel!* my boys!"

"If what I learn lodges them where they ought to lay their limbs, they will pipe another tune!"

Dismissing the bullies from his mind, since he was committed to the following up of this maze, he walked on in the dark, boldly, as if he were furnished with the Pope's *Salvus-conductus*, confirmed by the Duke of Guise, probably more efficacious on a safe conduct in this region than his royal master's.

Presently he was rewarded for his perseverance; he was in the fully-inhabited part of the mansion. It is true that no persons were about, but there were signs of many servants being here at the proper hours.

Corridors were faintly illumined by nightlights, wicks floating in bowls of tallow which their own heat turned into oil. He accounted for the absence of life by thinking that the concourse would be in the hall, and that the servant's not enlisted in the League would be sent to their quarters in the attic.

But there was nothing to detain him on the ground floor. He divined that in the cellars there would be no other attraction. He went

up the second stairs, not venturing on the grand
one, in the course of decorations, for the
painter's scaffolding was still up.

Here was the true house, the castle in a dwelling of mediaeval buildings; hard to reach, save
by the stairs, easily defended against a host.

It was complete—hall, chapel, dining and sitting-room, boudoir, storerooms, and a draw well
in a nook for supply of water out of an ever-
flowing well.

In this hall was no doubt the place of gathering. If he could but get in at its gallery, he
might hear all without being suspected.

Was this the sagacious plan of his correspondent and was he right in disbelieving that love,
save indirectly, had a hand in the invitation?

As he stood in doubt a scent was whiffed on
the air. It was so different from the usual reek
of the low-burning lamps that he was gratified;
but, what was more, he had recognized the odor.
It was that from the smelling-bottle of the
Princess of Porcian. At an era when each

high dame had a perfumer in her suite, or, at least, in her wages, and each prided herself on one or the other of the changes rung upon musk or civet, he might conclude that this aroma betrayed the proximity of the lady.

He felt his heart dilate; he forgot what was his errand; he darted briskly upon this trail, and, finding it left him at a door, was nearly inclined to put his shoulder to it and enter by main force.

Luckily, his ardor had not yet consumed all his prudence.

Certainly, the door had a keyhole, but the hangings within forbade an inspection of its interior. But the door was high—so high that the joiner had failed to attempt to make the panels reach all the height. Above it was, therefore, a little cross window, movable for shutting off the cold air in winter.

St. Megrin saw a footstool for the groom at the door to rest upon. Stood upon one end, it enabled him, standing upon it, to reach this cross window.   He did so, pried it with his dagger, opened it on its two horizontal hinges, and, with the dagger, cut a slit in the tapestry impeding a look beyond.

He uttered an exclamation of surprise and joy.

He slid to the floor and muttered:

"It is she!   It is the princess!"

It was she!   It was the lure!   Poor amorous pigeon!

CHAPTER XII.

BELEAGUERED.

As soon as Therine, Princess of Porcian, could cherish no doubt as to her being a prisoner in Soissons House, she mourned in secret. She dismissed everybody but her page, and only believed in him because he was a blood relative. Lady Cosse was discarded by her in a twinkling, for she saw that cupidity could make the senile creature betray youth and innocence for a paltry bribe. She believed that her letters to her father were intercepted. She feared that the enmity of Queen Catherine to the Duke of Guise did not lead a fair inference that she would busy herself for the foreigner of a race antipathetical to hers.

She felt so isolated that the absence of Arthur deepened her woe, much as the castaways despair when the last friend has been dispatched on a forlorn hope for succor.

So shortly, like a flower blasted by a sirocco, her charms appeared to flee. If health and mirth make beauty, then both these qualities were no longer hers. Mirth she did not try to call to her aid. It had fled the place, to lurk in the low drinking-place, from which she caught snatches of rollicking song and the clink of cups.

Health? She feared that would not long cling to her in this miserable state—a gilded prison. She saw she was incorrigibly pale, and that her brilliant gaze had become daunted and apt to lower. Her reverie was more miserable than her looking at the figures on the old arras, which presented elongated figures of hunters and naiads.

She had heard the servants whisper about a flight into the country, since there was a fore-cast of Paris delivered to the renewal of massa-cres for disputed creeds. In the country, still stranger to her than the town, she would be more than ever in the power of her betrothed.

Her last hope had fled in the ball being postponed, for she had determined to appeal to the ambassador from the Prussian provinces, which included her father's domain; to the first knight of the Teutonic Order; to the king or his gallants, whom she knew were hostile to her tyrant.

Now she was hopelessly immured, and her removal to another hold could not be resisted.

If she could correspond with that Count of St. Megrin! but her only confidant, Arthur, had incurred the ill will of her lord, and, he, no doubt, would never be suffered to approach her again.

Ruggieri, her neighbor—but she shrank from suing to that magi, whose horrid fellowship with the hated queen was famed throughout Europe.

She did not stretch out her hand to have a murderer's lead her out of even so burdensome a captivity.

She was drawn out of her melancholy mood by the striking on the church bells and the vague cry of the watchman.

"Half-after-twelve of the night!" said she, suppressing a tide of tears as she remembered how peacefully she would have been slumbering at home in her little white chamber on the banks of the Rhine; "how slowly the time drags, and yet I hate to lay down to court the rest which can never more be mine."

She was too proud to question the servants. She did not even look at those who entered for the regular duties. Lady Cross, offended by her overt treatment since she suspected her of double play, had prudently quitted her—forever, she hoped.

She had nothing to base any supposition upon; all she remembered was the Duke of Guise's dictation, based upon a meeting of his association in the neighborhood.

If, in spite of her refusal to write the decoy letter, it had been done by another hand, the Count of St. Megrin would by this have entered the trap.

"How vile is this prince?" reasoned she. "Is

he capable of rushing into my presence to tell me that the dripping blade he held was dyed in that gentleman's blood?"

So far, continued silence left her room for this fruitless sort of conjecture.

Then the storm overhanging Paris began to weigh on this quarter. She was nervous though it was not her nature. She had aches and pains without any cause or her ability to locate them. If she sat down, she was up and pacing the floor again and leaning at the closed window without caring if the blinds blocked the view or not. Only the distant lightning pierced them. But the boom of the thunder did not alarm her so much as the ignorance of what was going on concerning, not her, but the champion.

As for her oratory, with its shrine and praying stand, it offered no refuge—it would be no sanctuary, she believed, to the Duke of Guise, who was one of those bigots who shaped an idol to his ends—with his dagger, if need be.

In the midst of this fluctuating, yet acute, anxiety, she heard steps very faintly, but audible, at her door. She heard more noise at that door, the thin partition between her and this flimsy privacy! She looked up, and a glittering eye met hers, on high, in a rent of the tapestry.

More than the woman was roused in her—the insulted princess! She caught up a toilet pin and stood on guard. This door, fastened against her going out, opened more with force than skill, for St. Megrin had forgotten that he had been furnished with a master key—that is, as locks were much of the same pattern, the key he had would have opened this lock also. He had burst in, with the help of his dagger severing the bolt.

At this sight, too desirable to have been hoped for, her feelings were commingled so that she could appreciate none alone. Dismay, relief, apprehension, doubt, joy, grief!

On his part, he could only thank his good star, of which Ruggieri had not vaunted half the potency—this had guided him, spite of error, to her retreat.

"Let me hear your voice?" appealed he; "let me hear you give your welcome?"

"My voice? Oh, that can be used only to urge you to go away!" holding out both arms as to thrust him off.

"I was mad to believe in that international bombast—a conspiracy? Yet how could I believe in such rapture being mine?"

"Sir, regard your dire strait! If you opened that door, you can open others! Open them all and make away!" she said, lowering her voice, because the door was still open.

"Rash that I am!" He ran back and shut it. Then, perceiving a pair of firedogs at the fireplace, he lifted them, one in each hand, although massive iron and bronze, and wedged them against the closed door.

"Oh, will you not listen to me?"

"Forever! it is what I came to do," said he.

about to place himself on a hassock at her trembling feet.

"Do you not understand that the murderers let you come in but to immolate us together? Together! for your being with me would justify the bullet or the blow! Fly while you may! And yet by what way? for death is in every corner you were let pass! The assassins are posted everywhere!"

She imagined that she saw, with the clairvoyant's eye, the hidden slayers.

He threw down his cap, and ran his hand through his hair. The lock which he had shorn to leave a love token for her bristled up. He was afraid for the first time in his life, but not for himself.

It was not even his honor that was at stake, but hers!

He stared, stupified.

"What wild words are these on your lips? 'Assassin!' and 'death!'"

"Will you not hear me and dismiss this senseless delirium? In Heaven's name, will you not understand that this is not a question of life— yours or mine? You have been lured into an infernal plot! They will take your life, but they will take my fair fame!"

"They will kill me and not you?"

"No, they wish to send me home, flouted, scorned, to my father and my mother! Am I to cross the Blue River like a trullion—whipped on the ferryboat before all the neighbors?"

"A lure! Was not the letter of denunciation of treason penned by you?"

Her look of surprise and pain should have been her answer in full, but she said impressively:

"None such was from me." She showed her arm, black and blue. "No brutality, no torture, no violence forced me to write a word!"

The noble shuddered to see the bruise on the white arm, and then a glow of fire spread over him. Had the inflicter of that hurt been before him, he would have slain him at the foot of the crucifix of that praying-desk.

"Some other wrote the note—but the duke laid down the words."

St. Megrin tore up the paper, and set his foot on the shreds.

"It was by the duke, and I believed it—he thereby decoyed me not to a love-meeting, but to one of plotters against my king! And yet, why should I have believed that this lady would betray her lord? It could not be for love of me!"

"Now that you know all," said she, recovering her previous alarm, "you must flee, you see! Flee! I tell you again, this is a matter of life!"

He had not heard her—he only mused over the belief that he was not beloved. His hand seized his dagger, and very little more would be required for him to lacerate his arm, like hers in his frenzy. She saw his agony and she moaned a prayer, racked herself as never before in her exalted, passive, arcadian life.

"Do you mean my life is sought?" asked he with a dreadful laugh. "I do not swerve from taking it straight to my enemies, for I am but a flower, which you have plucked from the bouquet of life! Let me be rained down, leaf by leaf—all the bloom is departed!"

He went to the door and removed the irons mechanically.

"Farewell!" cried he, dolefully.

But the door would not open; in the interval, it had been securely fastened without. In their enrapt state, neither had heard the operation.

"Fastened!" said he, recoiling.

She had no doubt that there had been lyers-in-wait; it was known that the gallant was in her rooms! It was as much to ruin her as to kill the enemy that all this was done.

"If they will not let me run at them, let him come to me! Henry of Guise!" cried he.

"dastard, recreant knight, traitorous prince, come and meet me! Had you only the cruelty to mar a woman's arm! Try mine, torturer!"

He thundered with his fist on the door.

"Hold! peace! Oh, do not call! He will be sure to come!" shrieked she. "Soon—soon enough—all too soon!"

"Why should that matter, since I am indifferent to you? I do not say you are pitiless, too, but——"

"But if you would seek—if you would try—if you will aid me, you may avoid this lugubrious fate!"

"Avoid it! Avoid my doom, even though I am his peer!"

"His peer?" repeated she, thinking he was surely deranged.

"The king has made me a duke that I might fight him on even terms—it is he who has degraded himself below my former state, below a man's level, by this trap and this onset of murderers! He will come, no doubt, but you will see—not unattended!"

"Fly, fly!" reiterated she till hoarse. "Oh, think of the delicious daylight and the open fields!"

"I think only of the open grave! But it is not my corse alone that will fill it, heaven helping! But my death or my life are wholly as trifles, dust of those fields to you—fly! How fly from your coolness, your hatred, perchance!"

"Why do you think I hate any fellow-creature? Ah, would to Heaven that others loved as purely——"

"Oh, can you love? Then, under the heaven you appeal to, give me one word still! I will obey you blindly, then! Tell me, as heaven is above, and the grave at my feet—will my death here in your sight be more than the murder of any other man?"

"Great saints! do you ask me that? Oh, yes, it would! It would!" the cry seemed ex-

torted from her by a power overbearing her
faculties.

He saw that he was not deceived; that he
must forgive her—that she must forgive him
for having wronged her—that, in a word, he
was beloved.

His whole course changed. He would submit to evading the man he had challenged—or,
at least, his myrmidons.

"But as you speak of escape, what means
are there? That way?"

"Into my rooms—no outlet there!"

"Fly! a St. Megrin fly!"

"The assassins are hirelings—you are rich—
Geld reicht weit," she said in her native tongue,
"money will clear a road! Treat with the ruffians——"

"I descend to that! Never will I retrace
my steps since you love me!"

"That is why you must be gone. You are
not fleeing before that rocky-hearted prince,
but before a host of assassins. This meeting

of Leaguers was to sacrifice you! Even now
he is placing them at all the issues—they will
storm as on a fortress. Yet——"

He had made the circuit of the room, trans-
formed into a lion, whose walk, when enraged,
his resembled; he listened, he searched, he
scrutinized the air—he reckoned up all the pos-
sibilities.

Doors and windows closed and guarded,
there was yet one egress—the chimney.

CHAPTER XIII.

IN THE SNARE.

But, as might have been also expected, the ease with which this communication with the open air could be utilized had occurred to the tenants; iron bars of great solidity crossed at two places, above the mantel and at the orifice; possibly, a boy might have glided through the interstices, but a man was debarred.

St. Megrin withdrew his head from the fire-place with a sigh; the glimpse above of the midnight blue sky had tantalized him.

He looked disconsolately at the lady, who was stupor-stricken; her head was splitting from the tossing of her frenzied brain; her thoughts were simply clashing.

He tore down the curtains of a window; it had no shutters without; they were unfixable at that height and over the old ditch. Nothing but a diving-bird could have taken that plunge.

He would simply kill himself or be lodged in the mud.

Then, since his death was a certainty, he thought only of retaliation—revenge!

Like a soldier on the battle eve, he ran his hand over his body; he tightened his belt, and loosened his sword. His dagger was blunt; he gave it a new point by thrusting it in a door keyhole, which, though locked without, might be opened there, and broke off the point in it to prevent any use of the instrument.

He stood on the alert, like a picket in advance, not doubting that he would be cut off.

On her part, Therine could only pray. She believed that all measures of the duke's vengeance had been fully taken. But she could not pardon herself for bringing about the destruction of the gallant man. He had come to her as a revelation of how unselfish true love could be. The fire of the Southron, unlike the Lorrainers' cautious fierceness, and meditated steps, struck her as a new kind of heroism un-

known among her pallid countrymen. She fell
on her knees, not to the shrine but to the de-
fender, who must fail even to defend himself
against such odds. She craved his forgiveness
for what part she had unwittingly, or, at all
events, unwillingly played to attract him into
the pit of death.

But before he could stammer a word, for her
beauty in such acute distress pulled at his heart-
strings, she sprang up.

A high and fiery resolution infused her—she
wished now to die with him, not with him pro-
tecting her, but beside him, receiving a wound
or two destined for her companion.

The cavalier led her to a chair, and she sank
in it.

It was he who knelt at her feet; as a wor-
shipper dies, kissing the idol, he felt that death
would come to him tenderly thus, under her
soulful eyes. This was more than pity.

"In few words," said he, softly, "tell me that
you love me! Not for what I have said to

you—that is little! Not for what I have done for you, for that is again so little! but for what I should have done! It is a man standing in the grave, of which he makes the last entrenchment, that addresses you. I speak to you as one dying."

Indeed, she forgot she was a princess; she became purely a woman.

Prejudices of her exalted station and her secluded life disappeared, and social ties snapped before this solemn pledge of his devotion, to be sealed with his best blood. He was going to die for her as one dies for his queen and country. It would be in perfect justice to surround his last moments with some of the heavenly felicities in the gift of the woman adored.

If she could have put the speech upon his lips, she would have promoted the one he breathed, with his eyes, dark and liquid as black pearls, bent upon hers.

"Ah, tell me that you love me!"

She did not hesitate or trifle now. She not

only answered to his wish, but added that she had believed him dearest from when she had seen him, on the Rhine, before she could dream that their lives were anew to cross, and, as it seemed, be cut short at the same instant.

She told him what he, in his ignorance of woman's feelings, could never have divined. How she had had many conflicts with herself on keeping to her rooms at Paris, when, had she gone into the court circles open to her, thanks to her being the old queen's ward and godchild, she might have come into nearness to him so often. But she had remembered the bonds imposed on her by her folk, and shunned even the hearing of his voice. She had followed his swift rise at court, his advance by great strides in the king's favor; she had been proud when she heard him cited as worthy to enjoy a monarch's confidence; one who would not aid him to waste precious time in foolery and worse! She accompanied him, mentally, in his own flights of ambition, as now he learned. Like him, she had pictured St. Megrin's lord as a statesman—a counsellor, an adviser—not a companion in ignoble sports and light pursuits.

But in her enforced solitude, she had been pursued by remembrance of his voice and glances, and the image which monopolized her field of view.

"Hear me without interruption of your own," breathed she, so lowly that half the time he had to imagine the sense of words which he but faintly heard.

Alas! both awaited interruption from without.

"Yes, yes, it is you I love! Here, in these rooms, I have peopled the loneliness with multiplications of your dear form! I have drawn apart to seek isolation, but you still appeared, and it was your intangible hand which checked on my lips the utterance of despair! On my lids, the tears of disappointment and repining. In the silence, voices spoke—or only one repeatedly, yours so mild, sweet and gentle!

Your eyes illumined the dark deeps! Paul,
then, I feared not to look toward you—to answer you directly. That spiritual likenéss of
yours knew, then, what now it knows by hearing! Those spells of seclusion, incarceration
in a silken prison, they were, though my childhood was serene and modestly joyous, the most
enjoyable of my short and cheerless life!"

He leaped to his feet, glowing, shining, and
agitated like one thrown out by a volcano. He
no longer agreed—would not submit to this laying down of his life as a few moments before.

"Malediction!" cried he, "this is the dame to
live for! Am I to quit here all the happiness
life can offer, the choicest earthly blessings, and
go into the hell which murderers and cowards
alone deserve! Say no more—repeat not that
you love me! Had you been hateful, proven
cold, I should have braved their point and edge
as for any lady in sorrow! but now, look at me!
I fear that I am afraid! Be still—oh, say no
more in the vein which makes one cling to life!"

"Paul, would you blame me—would you curse me!"

"I can curse the love which gives me a glimpse of heaven, and then tears me aloof! No, no, let me go to the death and fray like a soldier who just earns his pay—and tell me that I perish not in illusion and deceit!"

"There is no illusion!" said she, sadly. "Hark! on all sides! They come! There is no deceit!"

St. Megrin drew the blade, holding which his predecessor in the royal bounty had lost his young life, not for a worthy woman, but for a worth-little king.

"You should withdraw," said he, with gentle firmness, "for you would unman me! I would not have you see me weak, palsied, cowering—sooner, look on your knight dead! Be off, for these oxen are about to run up against a mountain!" He appeared to increase in bulk as well as height, his long sword became a lance. His flashing eyes, firm-set mouth, dilating nos-

trils and bristling hair presented a more appalling spectacle than the head on Perseus' shield.

"You speak well," said she, hanging her
head. "I will go into the oratory and pray to
heaven. Except from above, we can await no
relief!"

At the moment when there was the buzz and
scuffle of many feet like hunters gathering
around a lair, a sound at the fireplace called
their eyes thither. A shapeless object, like a
coil of serpents, had fallen down the smoky
tunnel, and lay on the stones, vibrating with
the shock of the fall.

St. Magrin rushed upon it with avidity.

"A rope," said he.

He looked up in the channel. The square of
blue sky was partly cut off; a solid obstacle
barred out the view of a star—St. Megrin's
star, which the astrologer had pointed out.

He could not discern a form, but he heard a
voice descend:

"Are you there, lord count? Have you the rope?"

"It is Arthur!" cried the lady, having placed herself at the same recess.

"Your page—that was your page? This is true work if the letter was a snare!" said he, taking up the rope.

"Arthur!" said the princess, piteously.

The page had heard her sigh ascend, for he replied:

"My lady! still alive? Bless you! You are beset! They are in hundreds! Woe! I cannot slip through—there are strong bars!"

"Save yourself!"

She spoke none too soon. A shot was heard from a firearm. It was clear, by the boy being seen upon the housetop, that armed lookouts were posted in high places on the buildings around about.

"Hundreds," repeated she, wringing her hands. "Is he killed?"

They heard a laugh in a youthful voice, free from care and fear. And the same voice sang defiantly as the singer, no doubt, scrambled over the parapets.

> "You are wasting your powder—
>   You are wasting your shot!
> The sparrow of Paris
>   Is not for your pot!
> The hail may repel,
>   The snow cramp the wing,
> But the sparrow'll return—
>   I'll be back in the spring!"

"I recall it now," said the princess, somewhat relieved in that quarter. "There is a balcony under this window. You might slide down there and thence to the lane. On the ground——"

He had gone to the window indicated, with the beneficial rope. It opened on the void. No shot was fired—he did not perceive a gun-match burning in the intense blackness; he was staring into a gulf.

At all risks he fastened the rope at one end to the leg of a massy buffet and threw the other

part out. Its weight brought it out to its full
length. It did not seem to reach any foundation, but it was uncaught by anything.

"Will those cursed doors hold out!" muttered he, for the enemy, aware that the shot
told the whole neighborhood of the assault, as
well as the person aimed at, had with one impulse flung themselves at all the doors and casements they could attack.

Not only did the woodwork bend and spring,
but axes showed their crescent edges through
the first clefts they made.

Therine had thrown herself against the
door by which her gallant had entered, for she
heard a well-known voice urging on his
janissaries.

"Down with it, as with him!"

"Guise!" said St. Megrin. "Ah, coward, is
it thus he would disable me from meeting him
in the duel? Oh, coward knight! Oh, un-
principled prince! He should end on the gal-

lows! He ought to be on the end of this rope!"

He saw that she was in dire peril, for a spear-head pierced the fractured panel.

"Come away—rather my death than saved by such a buckler!"

"Open, lady of mine!" cried the duke, sar-castically; "open, as you are worthy of the honor promised you!"

"Wait, I shall open to you!" said the count, turning to the shivered door.

"No," said the princess, dragging him away so that they should not be seen together rather than to avoid the possible shot, if a firearm was thrust in at the opening where the spear had entered. "You will save more than your life or mine by flying! If you stay, I swear to die before you—on your breast, and that will be dishonor to Therine of the Clèves! Fly——"

"Without you?"

"Without me, but with all my love!"

"A ram—a battering ram!" yelled the furious

duke; "ply the hatchets, you numb-fingers! Strike with the butt of the halberds! At a siege you would but give the garrison time to man the walls! Down with this sheet of paper! Or lend me your axe!"

CHAPTER XIV.

FRIEND INSTEAD OF FOE.

The din was terrific.

Therine threw her arms around her lover and embracing him, murmured:

"Away! Farewell! Away!"

"Yes, away it is! But I shall make him remember this!"

"Aha!" shouted the duke, spying the gallant. "He is here! Oh, this is where the hare got the pepper thick!"

"Catch the hare and find it a wolf!" retorted St. Megrin, but nevertheless he rushed to the window where the rope trailed rigidly now.

One would think a weight had been appended to the end.

The count peered out, but could see nothing. He put his sword crosswise in his teeth, and thrust one leg over the sill to step out.

Before him the top story of an old wing of

the first Soissons House loomed up closely and overhanging; luckily, it had remained dark and silent. He had not believed an attack would also emanate from here too; it seemed too cruel to be encompassed in every part.

But over against a window, long since sealed up and grimed and gumed with dust, opened with a powerful impulse from within.

A brilliant flame from one or more torches showed in the garret, among suspended sausages and hams, and sweet herbs drying, several armed men, with their swords bared. They advanced to the window, which they had broken open. The torchlight fell past them into the chasm under the other window. St. Megrin, glancing down, saw that on the balcony indicated by the princess two or three men were grinning as they held the rope. If he did not descend by this means into their midst they could mount by it, and would fall upon him perhaps at the same time as the Duke of Guise's party burst into the room.

"Hemmed in!" muttered he, literally seeing foes before him, beneath and all around.

He glared down, spellbound, when one of those below looked up. He recognized, by his peculiar beard and his likeness to Henry of Guise, the Duke of Mayenne, his brother.

Mayenne must have known him, for he said, throwing his words upward:

"Mark, count and duke, there is no quarter!"

He receded. The men before him had not been idle after recovering from the shock of finding the window left them on the brink of the abyss which had daunted St. Megrin to some degree.

They had drawn back from the gap, but it was to take up two of those poles which purveyors carry a string of rabbits and hares on to the cook-shops; they thrust them over the space, burst in the two folds of the windows which St. Megrin had opened, as if to facilitate their entrance, and two, in single file, with infinite daring, advanced over the narrow and springy bridge.

The count reckoned two as no serious obstacle. He chose this attack at the weakest point. Hence, it would be his place to drive the wedge.

He leaped upon the window sill, and brandishing his sword prepared to spit the first comer, hurl him down upon the wretches below, and at once perform the same feat upon the next one.

But to his extreme surprise, this advancing swordsman, stooping to keep his weight concentrated and gracefully balancing himself, uttered in a low voice:

"Don't be a fool! Would you transfix your best friend, count?"

"Bussy! Bussy of Amboise!" ejaculated he, the sword almost falling out of his hand with glad amaze.

"Yes; do you not want aid?"

He passed on and bounded into the room.

He found no one to receive him; for St.

Megrin had seen the door, most mercilessly beaten at, give way in long splinters. In at the gap, pushing the hanging pieces off the bent hinges, dashed a score of men.

The princess had run screaming into the oratory.

St. Megrin, without looking to see if Bussy, intruding so opportunely, was at his heels, darted at the foremost and began thrusting, parrying and cutting—for the sword was two-edged—like a madman rather than a fencer of any set school.

He had to do with slashbucklers also, of every school or of no school but that of tavern skirmishes and bagnio battles. Bussy, taking the foe in the flank, had no leisure to watch the other's fighting. It was worth seeing none the less.

Guise had come in with the second rush, but he had followed the princess into the oratory. Here he was himself besieged, as the little bridge over which Bussy had flown to the res-

"In at the gap—dashed a score of men."   See page 222.

cue was passed successively by his companions, who banged at the door to compel the duke to come forth. Others, on the window sill here and over there, rained down the furniture, stores and tiles upon the group around the Duke of Mayenne.

In the meantime, St. Megrin had broken his sword short off; he attacked with the stump in one hand and his dagger in the other, and these failing, he used the handles as a weight to his fist like the loaded gauntlet of the ancients. At the same time, Bussy gave him some relief. On this, he broke a leg off a chair and showered blow for blow, as if he had regained another spell of life.

"Keep it up!" cried Bussy, "I see that you have no fear of your life!"

He was so badly wounded that he had bound up his left arm, wrapping his short mantle around it, after a Spanish model, so as to parry with it.

Meanwhile, over the temporary bridge

poured the friends of Bussy. But then, the poles became disarranged, and, one falling, none but a rope dancer could cross on the single one.

Mayenne brought up his reinforcement through the house.

They repelled the king's men, and drove them out into the yard.

Here reinforcements came to the latter, but they could not re-enter for a time.

On doing so, with the aid of the frightened servants, they found the place empty of all but the dead and wounded. They had found the secret issue.

"But how came you in so providentially?" demanded St. Megrin, in a pause to deliberate on the next step, for the neighborhood was aroused and the place would soon be overrun with the watch.

"It is simple," replied St. Luc, who had well seconded Bussy.

As we have seen, the gallants had followed

the prowlers in the street to Grenelle, where they missed them. The bravos and leaguers had vanished as into the ground. For alleviation of the disappointment, they entered the wineshop which St. Megrin had remarked.

When the shot was fired, they linked it with the disappearance of St. Megrin, and while some leaped out into the street, others, with Bussy, went up into the attic, having received a hint from the wine-drawer that so the other house could be reached.

The smoke of battle had cleared.

"They thought, the Guisards," said Bussy, redressing his wound, "that they had you in their hands and could use you as they pleased."

"Yes, but the lady, the Princess of Porcian?" cried the gallant, who thought little of his rescue.

A servant related that the Duke of Guise had held out in the oratory until his brother penetrated to him. There they had united their forces. such as were unmaimed, and carried the lady off in their midst, by the unsuspected way which connected, it was now found, the new mansion with the old one, or at least, that part assigned to the magician Ruggieri.

This was confirmed by the little page.

Arthur descended from his perch, where he had seen at least the flight of the duke.   He was weeping over the abduction of his lady.

"Did any of you hear the duke say anything, which would furnish a clue to the route he follows?"

It could only be gathered that, humiliated and enraged by his double failure in influencing the king to appoint him commander-in-chief of the League, and at the miss-fire of the enterprise against St. Megrin, he had fled to his army.

He had left a kind of treasonable threat.   He was reported as to have said, in the hearing of one of his emissaries dying of a lunge from St. Megrin, that, "after the servitor he would deal with the master!"   That is, after having killed the count-duke, he would not shrink from removing the king by violence as impudent as this midnight outrage.

The triumphal gallants escorted Bussy and carried St. Megrin through the streets in the dawn, making the old house fronts ring with their cheers, and execrations of the fled duke.

Henry heard the story as soon as he awoke, and remarked, with a sly smile:

"He will not meet St. Megrin in a duel, Epernon, have no fear. Come and partake of my *pogge*—of which I will send a slice to St. Megrin. I will do him the politeness to suppose that he is taking to the field, and that I may meet him in the battle."

"I do not think so," returned the baron.

"If, however, they cannot come to terms, I believe that I shall send him an antagonist whom he will not flinch from."

"Oh, oust him from that preference!"

"You are too gallant toward such a foe! But

we are going to forestall Guise and Mayenne in their campaign! Will you come with me?"

"All! all!"

His surgeon sent word that he feared that he could not save St. Megrin. The king forsook everything and hastened to his couchside. He was sitting up, which he had no business to do.

"Sire, sire!" implored he, clasping his gashed and bandaged hands, "they tell me that at last you are going to take the field in person! It is well! Oh, give me leave to follow you! I shall get well enough to keep upon a horse, and, like the blind king, charge, if bound upon the saddle, into the ranks. But I do not want to charge blind—I must single out my foe—I must harry the duke so that he will not think of marrying!"

The king studied him; pale, shrunken in features, weak in voice; undoubtedly fevered.

"If he opposes me, he will be harried," replied he. "Go now, and rejoin me at the earliest," said he, soothingly. "If there is no hindrance to your own wedding, I shall dance at it yet!"

"Meanwhile——"

"The duke shall not marry in haste, sir! I will, if he comes under my hand, hold his! If he should marry in haste, as they say, he will be given no time to repent!"

His air of determination was similar to his minion's.

"We are going to hold the Parliament at Blois. Recover and come there. If the duke comes also, I promise you that postponement is not acquittal! He shall give you satisfaction, as arranged."

"He will now face you only on the battle-field!"

"Then we will corner him in, and there you shall chastise him, and deal him with this maimed hand the *coup de grâce!*"

The count smiled sadly, but thankfully, up to him.

"They all die mournfully that love me," said

the king. "Ah, I have a heavy debt to wash out in his blood! No, I do not think that that hand will punish him! but I can find one that will. Guise is very well as a traitor. He must die a traitor's death. Not on the glorious field in a flash of victory! not like he would have had me die, pining in the monastery, but as he treated Quelus and this young gallant—butchered. For this must be," concluded he, as he moodily reached his rooms; "for if he unites his forces with Henry of Navarre's, I shall be as the hare between the harriers and the fowling-piece!"

CHAPTER XV.

THE MAN WHO SOUGHT REST.

St. Megrin had been placed by his friends under the royal surgeon's hands; but as the king
made a very hasty departure from Paris,
which was deemed tantamount to a flight, the
surgeon, wishful to be miles out of danger, accompanied the court to Blois.

Thus the wounded gallant was left in the care
of the apothecary to the royal household, who
had had his sign painted out and "to the Holy
Union" substituted. This worthy truckler persisted that his patient was still far from con-
valescent, probably to augment his bill for med-
icines and board.

The patient returned that the fever was out
of his bones as regarded his hurts, but that it
was on the surface impelling him to action.

He had been haunted in his delirium by the
fight repeating itself, as well as the princess ap-

pearing, like a Druidess with flowing, golden hair, to encourage her champion.

So he rose, flung down his purse, disregarded the injunctions to do this and that to prevent his gashes breaking out, and proceeded to his banker. He found this gentleman about the only king's man left in town.

The king had taken his favorites and the court their followers.

The League reigned triumphant, but had no leader at all, for the Duke of Guise was gone, with his ensigns.

Paris was decidedly unsafe for the royalists.

Lampoons fluttered about with the autumnal leaves; they likened the weak Valois to Tiberius, Nero, Herod! Called him a pro-Lucifer. Children flourished the latest Paris "article of novelty," which dethroned the pith-gun—scissors imitating that pair with which the Duchess of Montpensier had threatened to cut short the royal hair as her brothers had to cut his life.

The roads were all unsafe, likewise; one way,

you would run into the landless and lawless, speeding to join Guise's army, to be reinforced also out of his principality.   Another, dissenters to the church, hastened to join Henry of Navarre, with likelihood of meeting his swelling hosts half-way to the capital.   Least in valor, but not in number, the lackeys, crumb-catchers and fawners were traveling toward the seat of the congress, which the king was to open.

St. Megrin had the privilege of the royal stables, but it was as empty as his ducal title; not a horse was left at the Louvre mews, as a few in the stalls were pledged to officials packing up what had not been carried away on the first party setting out.   These only waited for the tocsin to grumble over the town, to run after the king and court, while there should be left king and court between Hammer-Navarre and Anvil-Guise.

The count had to have recourse to the royal post.   He had no servant, as George had gone with the favorites, having missed touch with his master, and assured by them that he was not resting in town, although they did not fully understand what a lodestone the affianced consort of the Duke of Guise was.

Established by King Louis XI., the civil wars had canceled any postal improvements, so that he was six days reaching Orleans. It is to be granted, however, that the best horses had been carried on in the king's march, and had not been sent back, as common travelers are obliged to do. Everything was dear; the prices were high and the tavernkeepers saucy.

As for the prowlers, hedge-hiders, human dogs, who played the scavenger, they let St. Megrin pass as small game. He was pale, haggard, dragging of foot, attired sedately and carrying the famous long sword of Bussy, replacing Schomberg's, broken to pieces in the affray. His head hung miserably since he learned that the princess must have been carried off in the Duke of Guise's train. Either he or his brother of Mayenne must have taken her in charge for conveyance—whither?

On he trudged when he could not get a horse, supported by hope, the lover's staff.

At Orleans he heard that Guise had conferred with his chiefs of the army, and local, and then quitted all to go to Blois. People laughingly and knowingly said that if the King of Navarre would also transfer his command of his army to a subordinate and attend the session, there would be "loggerheads (Henries) three!"

Mayenne had disappeared, probably being with the lieutenant-general of the League and the army of the east. The lady was too insignificant among these high personages to be noticed. The roads were guttered and rutted with innumerable vehicles of all sorts, farm carts being pressed into service, so that the gentry and nobility should get to the city.

St. Megrin was at a loss; it was not likely that the Princess of Porcian's warders would let her direct them to this common goal, so that she might lay her plea for release before the estates of Blois!

As well turn one way as another until something definite was come upon. There was a slight comfort in the lady not being possibly accompanied by the duke himself in his daring movement to beard the Valois in his stronghold. Dismissing the love-chase for the moment, he determined, by the smarting of his cicatrizing wounds, to make good his challenge on his unknightly opponent.

For two stages, he had the luck to hire a jade and a nag, similarly spared from the crows to serve to catch a louis or two.

But the last, while munching a handful of oats at the inn of Deep Well, a paltry hamlet straggling along the road at a forks, was gobbled up as a pack horse by the baggage train of Lord Coesme, brother of the Countess of Soissons, traveling like a king, and replacing foundered horses at the expense of any one his high-handed lackeys met. St. Megrin could hardly appeal to his lordship on the grounds that he had been nearly murdered under his roof. Besides, Coesme was a Leaguer and more likely to be hurrying to Blois to support Lorraine than France.

There was a little heat already about his censuring the king's gallants, and so—not to be thumped by the servants' canes, the count prudently let himself be robbed and watched his last aid be whipped off.

The captain of a stranded ship looks naturally to the rock which split him.

St. Megrin saw the most dilapidated and unaccommodating of hostelries, without a name, indicating, by a green bush, now in the sere, that it sold wine. But the barn was immense, and the landlord was an important farmer and grazier. He had servants of robust and stalwart proportions, whom no one had tried to impress into their service as they had done the horses. The inn had no lodgings to offer. The vagrants, poachers, ragged outcasts, contentedly clustered around it, accustomed to the sky for coverlet, provided they could get a cup from the wine casks within the cellars.

Such as the hovel was, it had been wholly absorbed by a party going toward Nevers, they said. As this was the Protestant rallying point, St. Megrin believed that he had fallen in with Protestant squires eager to diminish their distance between them and the Valois, as well as the rabid Guise.

He scrutinized them; they were military and guarded a very military chest, but they had also in charge a lady, having maid and page, which suggested anything but a military expedition.

He inquired about her, which was natural in a young gentleman, while to do so about the escort might bring questions upon him.

The inn servants reported her fair as the Lady of Mayday, and blonde as the Siren of the Rhine; also, by her accent, a German, the landlord knew, as his tramps with cattle had taken him over the Rhine. The inquisitive young gentleman must not hope to see her, as she kept her room and wore a mask, too. Her maid was a Parisian, but not loquacious, which belied her extraction; as for the page, a pretty mannikin, he acted like Hector in the bud, flashing out a waspish dagger at every attempt to be familiar with him.

A German was likely to be a Reformer. But still this did not assure one that she was bound back to her own country or to the Protestants' flying camp. This was reported to be at Epinac, or even at Dijon, profiting by the Duke of Guise being to the west, and Mayenne being too fat to keep the field.

This steady northerly advance of the rebels favored the standard joke, which was circulating here, to wit, that Henry of Navarre would cast his vote at Blois. A deciding one.

This masked foreigner, worthy of a captain's guard, pricked St. Megrin's curiosity, or rather his love. But, on having one of her conductors pointed out to him as the chief, he felt almost sure that he was on the right track.

"Balzac of Entragues!" muttered he. "Antraguet is set aside by his lord—surely only to ward and watch over his betrothed.   Logically, this is the lady!"

Needless to say, he took very good heed that Antraguet should not view him in return. Moreover, he broke his plumes, slouched his cap, trusted that the sticking-plaster on his scarce-closed cuts would disfigure him, and tried to resemble the meanest of the refuse of the bivouac and forays.

If doubts remained, he soon had them set to rout.

He had boldly invited one of the guards of Antraguet to crack a bottle with him, on a pretended acquaintance founded in the Netherland campaigns.

Like the others, this was a *frei-ganger*, a free-goer, indeed, who held that law of nature that man had a right to all things; he was a "late-walker," one who preferred nocturnal attacks, who had sat oftener on "the Polish buck," or wooden horse, than a war charger; thirsty perpetually, he would have rubbed noses with a tinker rather than die "a dry death." He had a fluent reply to every question while the wine flowed.

Unfortunately, he had no true idea of their destination.

The lady might be on the way to east or south, only, as they were all true sons of the church, like the comrade with whom he was drinking, he did not believe that they would present her to Henry, the Huguenot, with his captain's compliments. As for that, she was beauteous and would tickle the well-known Evergreen Gallant's susceptible heart.

St. Megrin was convinced that only a mint would corrupt all the soldiers of this capacity— or a vault of the Orleans wine market.

He tested the louts to see if they could be mustered into a company of deliverance; they

were sharp as awls, brave with a club, but not
against swords; and pilferers ready with their
knives to saw half-through the baggage 'ropes
so that the packs might burst on the highway
and they have the pickings; but fight with them
—for a woman—never!

Besides, they were bigots and would not have
sided with an angel against the Duke of Guise,
brother of a cardinal.

As for the night-waifs, beggars asserting that
they had been prosperous farmers until burnt
out by the foragers, they were too few if they
could have been depended on to man a rush.

"Oh, for the Joyeuses, St. Luc or even Epernon—or for my formidable Bussy alone!"

Faithful squire, Antraguet was ever on the
lookout and he had to keep aloof. They would
have started overnight only for the lack of
transport.

"How nearly I missed her!" thought St. Megrin. "Misery as it is! To be near the unsteady court! If only I had a carrier to beg

the gallants to fly to me and peck!   Fatal night when we parted and I was parted from her—how cruelly I am walled off now!"

He had to lament until dusk.   Then, Antraguet took half-a-dozen men and went off to make a raid for horses, or scout before continuing at any hazard.

One of the remaining ones, with whom St. Megrin had struck up the bibber's compact, laughingly explained that he was gone to "borrow a saddle or two with four hoofs under the girth."

This was the chafing gallant's cue to procure an interview with the ward of Guise's factotum and confirm his more than suspicion.

But he had no more than entered the one reception-room, crowded to suffocation, before he feared that he was foredoomed to disappointment.   Assuredly to delay.

The law was being laid down without reckoning with the host, by the jack-in-office—that is, Antraguet's ensign.   His men had choked up all the snug corners and sat on the stair bottom, sprawling out their boots and balancing platter and pewter pots on their knees. This young, but hardened, scuffler refused entirely to let even the household go up into the upper story, as "his lady" should not be disturbed.

In vain the host, a pretty good arguer, with a poker in hand, as long as a sword and thrice as heavy, had claimed that he had not let to his superior a little cupboard which contained choice stores. He wanted it for a fresh-come customer.

This greediness grated on the nerves, however well tempered, of this mature, thick-set, inelegant but soldierly figure wearing dented and blackened half-armor under a weather-beaten horseman's cloak. He had stalked in like one who made an entrance by sheer force. He had come on a fine war horse, capable of carrying a ton, and of defending himself from "the lifters of cattle" by his own heels and teeth. But for the greater safety, the rider had en-

trusted him to a groom almost built after his re-
doubtable model. This man wanted not for
arms, to say nothing of a large-bore handgun,
swung at the saddle-hook.

Without a noble carriage, this intruder bore
himself like a man who, in the respects that he
most prized, had not yet met his more than
equal.

If not a courtier—he was born in a shield
and cradled in a helmet—that is, he belonged to
the camp.

The stalwart host had bowed to him more
lowly than to Antraguet and to Lord Coesme.
He recognized a man as strong as himself and
inured to vicissitudes of warfare out of his experience. This utter fearlessness was guided
by readiness of device.

The host offered him a corner, his last and
best, which he would not have done to the
Count of St. Megrin had the latter declared
himself the duke of the same place.

St. Megrin did not know this Brutus, who

had evidently been warring while he was at his studies, but he recognized the veteran who would go far under a leading spirit, and would, left at a breach, suffer himself to be hacked to pieces before they could clear the passage of him.

The gallant's ignorance seemed shared by the mercenaries and their present captain. This seemed to irritate him, though his was not vain-glory.

While awaiting the landlord's reply to his request for sleeping apartments, he seized a bottle, or rather a flagon intended to serve a whole table, and poured himself out a brimmer into a tall cup or rhinoceros hide mounted in gold, which could serve also as a powder-horn. He drank the dust off his mustache, and listened to the dialogue of the landlord and Antraguet's delegate.

The host, having been answered by the latter to the effect stated, turned to this overbearing

suitor and began an apology, which vexed the
other like a sailor who had counted on a sound
slumber after weeks on the tossing wave. He
listened with uneasy contempt, and overcast the
ensign and the pleader with his blackening
frown.

The landlord probably would not call his
staff—that is, the domestics, to his aid or the ensign's, who might reply on his armed force
alone. After all he would be but fulfilling his
orders and defending the lady's privacy.

The compact cavalier simply looked over his
broad shoulders out of the doorway, no doubt
to signal with his black eye to his follower. St.
Megrin, intercepting this glance, was impelled
by he knew not what—except enmity to anything in the colors of Guise—to return him a
nod of acceptance.

This was illustrated by the gesture of lifting
up his sheathed sword with both hands and ten-
dering it to him.

Gentlemen of the sword, both, sympathy was forthwith established.

Although one sword more or less does not seem much to precipitate an unequal encounter, yet the stranger assumed the air of one thoroughly assured of his having his own way now!

CHAPTER XVI.

"THE BRAVE CRILLON."

It was a crisis. To add to its intensity and so perplex the junior of the Guisards, the stranger's servant, inured to his master's habit of "not taking no for an answer," desiring no hint farther than that glance, had tied the two horses to the post-ring without. Dismounting methodically but briskly, he unhooked the short-barreled blunderbuss from its horn, and walked in doors like one called to a breakfast.

He uncoiled the match at his girdle, lit the loose end at the blazing kitchen fire without saying one "By your leave, my masters!" to those whose cheeks his hand roughly grazed, and wheeled round with the lint fizzing. He ranged himself close to his master. He was over-ready to support his demand, whatever it was, without asking its tenor.

At precisely the same nick, St. Megrin, although loth to be prominent, felt it his duty to place himself on the cavalier's left side. Instead of one person trying to browbeat a file of swordsmen here were three, each good of his kind, and self-satisfied that they could obtain elbow room anywhere and maintain it against odds.

On seeing this trebling of the foe, the ensign suddenly recollected that his captain's orders had been pivoted on the point of not making a noise about the lady. He drew the landlord aside and used him as a buckler while addressing him.

"Speak out, young man!" said the latter, but he listened to him.

Then he turned to the trio and said in a hearty voice, as if he would have been no oppositionist:

"The little closet shall be swept out and cleared, and a truckle-bed shall be stood up in it. Your honor cannot very well stand up in it, too, but it is long enough!"

He was sure that the newcomer would wring human neck or bottle neck with the same nonconcern, and so the other accepted this reply to his simple desire with coolness. But, while the sweeping and bed-furnishing was done, he showed that he did not care a whit that he had won his way over the young soldier, for, sitting down, he politely besought the volunteer aid to share the wine with him.

St. Megrin drew a chair from under a fellow slow to give it up and sat down with a corner of the long board between them, each having the sword-arm free. The host himself brought in a choice bottle. The warlike servant snuffed out his match, shouldered his gun and strode out, as if he neither regretted the incident nor its poor result.

But at the door he lit another, but mental, means of enlightenment, which produced a blaze of glory.

"May I never stir from a good supper but ye are all a troop of awkward riders! for not one of ye could have trod a field of battle not to hail the brave Crillon!"

He continued his exit without pausing to witness the prodigious effect of his simple speech.

To name Crillon between 1560 and 1600 was the same as saying Bayard at an earlier epoch. In a word, Henry IV., no mean judge of heroes, had characterized him, in presenting him to his wife, as "the foremost war-captain of the age!" "The Bravest of the Brave" was a Gascon. When it was suggested that he would be less of a bear if he learned to dance, he growlingly went to a dancing-master. But on his instructor speaking of "reversing!" and "retiring!" he protested.

"This will not do for Crillon! Know that the Crillons never retire and know not reverses!" It may be added here that when his body was examined by the doctors, over twenty wounds appeared by ineffaceable scars, and his heart was found twice the normal size.

Still, St. Megrin did not know this anatomical fact when he exclaimed, as the abashed crowd unanimously trailed outward at citation of this dread name:

"Oh, that great heart! You are Crillon? I am St. Megrin!"

"You, that I have heard of from Bussy! He styles you his brother, and the prompt way you sprang to my side proves that you warrant the term." He gripped the count's hand, which needed Guise's iron gauntlet not to become pulp; "I see that, like him, you do not count the odds when the scourings of the camp fall foul of a gentleman!"

"Bussy," replied the young man, blushing, "is my model for hand-to-hand encounters as you are for war! Ah, Bussy—you should have seen him in Paris there, when I was overrun by rats —he and the few gallants trod them under— twenty to a hundred and his arm in a scarf!"

He forgot his vexation, like the captain his, and they were joyous over the wine, which was really delicious.

Crillon poured out no news from Blois. Always taciturn, he was embarrassingly silent. His new companion did get an answer to questions, but they were meagre ones.

"You seem to need a bed badly!" said he.

"It is the first time in years that I shall repose on my own couch!"

"The deuce! Then you are not hastening to —to—Paris?"

"Paris is nothing to me, for I got out with difficulty."

"It was so with me. Going to the army of the league, without the walls?"

"No, and yet they would embrace a red-hot Catholic. But it is dissolving for want of that cement called subsistence money! Unless he captures the king's treasurer and diverts the coin from the favorites' toys—no offense—he will find his noble cavaliers and stout pikemen dispersed like snowflakes in the spring breeze!"

"Well, a fervent Catholic will not be going to

coalesce with Henry, the Huguenot," said the other, merrily.

"I do not say that! Creed has nothing to do with it. My sword is as good without the cross-bar. I seek service since my bones ache in unwonted rest, and I will accept it under a king who keeps sword and torch bright and lets the assassin's dagger rust."

"Eh? I know one Prince Henry who uses that—and on my own criss-crossed skin!" He tapped two or three scars on his neck and wrists. "The Guise! whom you have just quitted at Blois, no doubt, where he awaits me to carry out our solemnly arranged duel."

Crillon looked around the deserted room. The fugitives had assembled around the beggars' fire and only a few peered in at the open windows, as if on a wild beast, which might yet leap out at them if teased.

"He is not thinking of a single combat—but of a number of them. He has his hands full of that figure of birdlime called the Valois. Pah!"

"Halloa! Have you fallen out with the king?"

"I am afraid that I shall be besmirched if I stick to him! You do not know the king yet, young sir! Well, then you will never guess what he called me into a private audience for?"

"At Blois?"

"In the castle, where he is the host, of course! He proposed, as I would, a toast to your health! He asked me—(he gagged as if a fragment of cork was choking him)—me to assassinate his guest in cold blood."

"His guest is—Guise?"

"The duke with the scar! yes. 'The staff has been broken on him;' he is doomed—but treat a ducal criminal properly! Slay—do not stab! It was bad enough that Condé, who tried to abduct Henry, should be treacherously done to death, but it was on the battlefield—the murderer, if it were murder, as I think, risked his life all sides. but—assassinate after dinner in his own bedroom—hold! It makes me queasy!"

"Did you reply?" asked St. Megrin, dwelling on the answer as if it might mar his hopes.

"With an effort! Lord knoweth how it was I did not throw my guards' surcoat at his crown, but I replied, civilly and respectfully, for he still bears the sceptre of France: 'Sire, you mistake your man (historical)!'"

"Scurvy!" remarked his hearer, as if forced so to comment.

"That scalded his ear! So I am going, after the repose I earned in that dishonorable service, to join the King of Navarre, who is a Bourbon and hates assassination as he does a Lorraine!"

"But he is chief of the Reformers——"

"Oh, let him reform the church at the last —reformation of other things will take him all his life! Did I not say that creed is nothing when peace and country are at stake? This descendant of St. Louis is a true king, and you will see that, young sir! Live long and your eyes will see him crowned at Rheims for the whole of united France!"

"So be it," said the count, draining his glass, quietly.

Probably enraged by his latest favorite being traitorously dealt with at Paris, Henry had resolved to punish Guise with his own captain's sword.

"It was only the mode, then? If the king had set you on the prince in a fair fight?"

"As he did you? Oh, Guise would naturally, and by bounden duty, refuse! What the plague! a general has no right to fight with even his peer when the enemy's line of battle confronts his own. He might have thrust me aside to go and meet King Henry of Navarre."

St. Megrin heard this lecture with a kind of shame.

But he was given no time to raise objections, as there was an alarming clatter of hoofs on the highway.

He sprang up, as he believed that Antraguet

had raised an accession to his body, and, as he would recognize him as the king's minion, he would be cornered even more tightly than Crillon. But the cry without was "For the king!" The whole reined up at the door, where, installing themselves with excellent precision, outlet was not left. Even more, two or three, carrying firearms, raised them and threatened the upper windows, where, no doubt, curiosity had brought unwanted pryers.

CHAPTER XVII.

FOR THE KING.

Crillon rose and looked out of the open doorway.

"Whew! how close upon me! It is Baron Vitry!"

"Your own lieutenant of the Bodyguards?"

"Oh, he becomes captain now by my resignation. Come to lug me back to the king, have they? Know they not that Crillon resistant requires a crane! Only ten or so—the king still rates me cheaply. Well, young lordling, I cannot suppose the darling of the king will again stand by me to stay me from occupying that bed which the king assigns me in Blois dungeons?"

"God forbid!" cried the other, but he hardly could support this rebel.

"Is it eschew or embrace?" asked he.

While Crillon hesitated to form a plan of resistance, Baron Vitry entered. Over his breastplate and other warlike accoutrements he wore the surcoat with the flower-of-lilies, which denoted that he was acting on the king's immediate service.

Having seen Crillon's servant and the horses at the door, he had no doubt he had attained his goal. He saluted him with a coldness of bad augury.

"I warn you, baron, that I shall give up my sword, which is the king's gift, but not my person!"

"It is not I who want your company, but the king," returned Vitry, like a soldier who still deferred to his ex-superior. "Keep the sword, and if it be until he finds another such hand to sway it, I shall not be captain long! It will not be among his boyish gallants, although they promise some good lately!"

"Ha, ha!" said Crillon.

"I thank you for them, baron!" said St. Megrin. "Don't mind me!"

"Oh, ho! you are here? I thought you, ruffler, had been smoothed out in a riot at Paris and now dwelling leagues beyond man's life. Excuse me farther congratulations—but my word is with Crillon."

The two stood aside, and St. Megrin, looking at the stairs, now unguarded, itched to bound up them.

"Not for the marshal's baton!" replied the discharged captain to a proposition.

"But if——"

"There are no ifs and buts in me. Not to exchange that blade for the sword of state!" replied Crillon in the same firm, yet offended tone. "Never would it be cleansed!"

"Pest upon this stubborn fit. Let me have something shaped like an answer to take back to his majesty!"

"Oh, you can take a plainly shaped answer! Since he will not let me sleep in peace and free, I go for another lodging than under his roof.

To the castle of Blois or the Louvre Palace, I choose the tent of his brother Henry."

He bowed curtly, stepped out of doors and mounted his horse, which the groom began to untie. He rode off a little space to make sure bit and bridle were in order, while Vitry, chop-fallen, came also to the outlet. Returning to caracole and rein up the steed, Crillon said in a ringing voice:

"This to the king: It was Crillon who cried out: 'Long live King Henry the Fourth!'"

"You saucy rebel!" shouted Vitry, as well as he could for laughing. "Present pistols, men!"

Soldiers are not full of alacrity when a fatal order concerns their old officers. These brought their pistols to bear with no surprising swiftness, and the wheel which carried the steel teeth against the set flint over the powder pan revolved slowly. Still, they presented arms at the fugitive, who nobly swerved a little to prevent his groom being a bulwark.

"Take aim, fire!" roared Vitry, with seeming good faith. But St. Megrin, by his rear, distinctly heard the postscript, namely: "Miss him, you bunglers!"

"I shall like this Vitry baron for that!" muttered he.

The volley was therefore sheerly a salvo of joy.

This detonation, none the less, was a great cause of consternation in and about the house. Antraguet, returning, believed that there was an outbreak among his mercenaries or with them. He hurried on his steps, wondering if the Huguenots had taken the village, from the still echoing warcry in Crillon's stentorian voice:

"Long live King Henry the Fourth!"

He did not for an instant believe that his Henry was intended.

On seeing the royal guards at the doorway and two officers, as well as he could make out, between the jambs, he prudently altered his course and ran in with his followers at the back through the scullery.

St. Megrin looked at Vitry dubiously.

"It is a fair notice," said he. "He has gone to join the rebels—he told me he would."

"He will, and it is a great loss! This puzzles me, for I wanted such a man."

"You! He?"

"Did he tell you what he refused——"

"To execute an order!"

"To execute a man!"

"Yes!"

"Then the order devolves on me, his lieutenant. But he refused more—he refused the marshalship of France!"

"Then this man——"

"France's highest prince—and the king's lowest foe!"

"My own—Guise?"

"Ah! that is so. Well?"

During this colloquy, rapidly spoken, Antraguet had resolved on a dash. He must have run up the stairs, for over the two gentlemen's heads, they heard the folds of a window open and a head was thrust out, for a woman's voice shrieked:

"My mistress! they are dragging my mistress hence, *nolly-volly!*"

It was Marie, whose knowledge of dog-Latin allowed her version of "nolens-volens!"

Both turned around. Steps were heard on the landing above. They expected, after this announcement, to see a man or two carrying down a lady, but, instead, was a fair boy, with his long locks streaming, who descended the steps as a boy would, three or four at a time.

"Help! help!" his flute-like voice, hoarse with emotion. "They are bearing away the Princess of Porcian!"

St. Megrin had his sword unsheathed in a flash. He parried two strokes with which as many ruffians tried to cut down the boy.

"Warring with children after women!" said he. "The princess! You are still her page, Arthur!"

"Oh," cried he, in the utmost surprise and

joy; "it is the count—the Count of St. Megrin! Then, my mistress is saved!"

Antraguet appeared at the top of the stairs, quivering with the firm step of St. Megrin upon it.

"A word will frustrate that," returned he. "This way, Guise and Lorraine!"

A rush of the mercenaries hedged in St. Megrin and Vitry, carried to the stairway foot. Vitry set his back against his companion's so that they faced each way and had the foe repulsed.

"Two words to that," said he; "here, Valois and France!"

The baron had really no choice about his course. With an order to make away with Henry of Guise, his followers were included. Besides, he knew that King Henry had never held any favorite so dear as this St. Megrin, whose absence preyed upon him, and he believed that it was not slightly to avenge him

"A rush of the mercenaries hedged in St. Mergrin and Vitry, carried
to the stairway foot."   See page 267.

that he had sentenced his disappointing antagonist to death.

It was a three-sided contest. Antraguet had
the upper hand in one sense, but he stood alone
between the two women. Below him, he saw that
the king's troopers, chosen men, were capable
of devouring his corps. Besides, these hirelings, hearing that the Lorraine treasury was
hollow, wished to be on the side which would
furnish clothes and food for the coming winter.
Indeed, half of them left the others and quitted
the kitchen, too. The others were opposed by
the guards entering in their full force.

"Down points!" shouted Vitry, clapping
his hand, with the sword hilt in it, on his chest
where the royal arms were blazoned. "Do you
not know that during the parliament there is a
God's truce! Strike and break it, and my word
will be 'The next tree!'"

The enemy quailed. They knew perfectly the
signification of that gesture.

"*Sneck up* is the word!" was passed among

them, and Antraguet saw from his eminence that half these few were dropping off.

St. Megrin had a flash of genius. Love must have inspired him, for he caught a glimpse of a precious form above, and a gleam of flaxen hair over Antraguet's scowling features.

"No blood need be shed," said he, "between gentlemen who understand one another. I am the Count, ay, Duke of St. Megrin! I engage you who are not traitors to the king to escort this lady still, only in the name of Queen Catherine, who is her god-mother."

The men conferred and their self-elected chief, treating the ensign as a boy of no position, stepped forward.

"Here is my purse as earnest."

Money shines never dimly—the man's eyes glittered and his friends caught the gleam.

The count smiled at his success. He drew out of his secret pocket in his doublet one of those drafts which the Jews had long employed to circulate the scanty cash.

"Two of my friends, your gentlemen, baron, shall captain these worthies. This draft will be honored as they call it, by Alaezar at Strasburg——"

"In the Jewry, by the bridge of boats," said one of the guards, who was a Swiss.

"Or, which is the same, if you can reach Clèves, it is her father's! This is the Princess of Porcian!"

Therine, sublimely ignoring Antraguet, whose fang had been drawn, descended the stairs as if the approach to a throne. She had so queenly and calming a bearing that all doffed their hats or saluted with their swords. Antraguet alone let her pass with sulkiness.

Therine had the tact not to single out her deliverer for all her gratitude, and Vitry might well imagine that he was esteemed the higher for lending her two of his men and the confirmation of St. Megrin's arrangement.

The royal guards escorted her, with maid and page, to the litter brought around to the door,

Antraguet's best horses were harnessed to it, and the party were given a cheer as they took a good start over any possible pursuit. Antraguet withdrew with the handful of men clinging to his drooping colors.

"He will see his master, no doubt," said St. Megrin, still staring up the road in the deepening dusk without spying anything of the white handkerchief lately waving.

"He will arrive too late, unless we are shamefully behind-hand," observed Vitry.

"Take me to where the duke is, and—our duel shall this time come off!"

"Duel? Nay; the king wished us to attack him in overwhelming force!"

"Listen," said the other, laying his hand on his arm and speaking with great gravity; "one of my ancestors was friendly with the Scotch Archers of the royal guard. They used to tell of a great lord being done to death, but one of the slayers, having doubts, left the band to return on their bloody steps. They asked him why he had returned, and he said, in their tongue: "To mak' siccer!"

"To make—secure? is it?"

"That is the meaning! Well, you may rest on it—I shall make sure!"

"I must not doubt you, but——"

"Take me to face him! You may finish what is left of him!"

Vitry eyed him up and down like a sergeant scrutinizing an offering recruit; then said he to himself:

"Though Crillon declines, all goes well, my promotion on it! This court-fop will die on his man!"

CHAPTER XVIII.

THE STAIN ON CASTLE BLOIS.

There are times when ambition, like love, blinds a man as well as makes him deaf even to the most piercing voice.

The Duke of Guise, who might have been safe with his forces, having the assurance that he could fall back upon very cordial Paris in event of a disaster, of his own volition, quitted all to attend the estates meeting at Blois.

His intimates, most of them preparing for their own retreat in case Henry of Navarre continued his entrance into France, advised him to fly! He ceased to listen to the warnings.

His brother, the cardinal, prayed him to break off in this odd resolve to turn the governing classes into his favor.

"You will be tripped up by some ignoble device," said he; "you will fall, my dear Henry!"

"I throw back to you your own words when

I urged you to keep out of Paris: 'The only fall man should dread is that from grace!'"

"Amen! It is not for me to doubt the universality of that grace, but I do doubt that Henry of Valois exists within the touch of angels' wings!"

The cardinal-duke, overwhelmed with presentiment, accompanied him to the risky rendezvous.

But, on seeing the high turrets and majestic portals of the ancient castle, he shuddered and vowed that he would have none of the royal hospitality. He went and lodged in the town on the steep street climbing up to the citadel.

On the contrary, his brother seemed eager to accept the king's especial hospitality.

Needless to say that it was difficult for a warrior to carp at the preparations lavished on his suite of apartments, making him feel as if Henry had brought the Louvre down and emptied its treasures of garnishment and furniture to do him honor.

It is hard to realize the gorgeousness of a mediæval residence on looking, as now, at the denuded walls, the faded drapery, the cracks and shrunken doors and windows. Then, the tapestries were new and bright; the chairs cushioned and lined with velvet well wadded; the little conveniences which luxury's ministers found then have disappeared so that the antiquarian hardly more than suspects their prevalence.

The pictures were built in the solid walls. The screens, to keep off currents of air, the ventilators working by turnspit dogs or by the variations of temperature, have rusted in place, and the dogs have long ago fed the crows.

If the guests' servants trod on rushes and sweet herbs gathered and thrown down daily on the floor, the masters had oriental rugs and squares of thick carpets to rest upon.

The lounges were roomy, even when heaped up with hassocks. Footstools were for each person.

Henry III. had introduced many refinements, such as the personal drinking-cup, which even the rude Crillon had adopted, as well as the fork of silver and of several prongs, instead of the cooks' which was of steel and had but two.

Blois was not quiet or gloomy during the session. The place became blithe and overrun by the numberless servants of the great lords and the boors attracted to town, the gypsies and other amusement mongers whose guitars, mandolins, tabors and fifes formed at least enlivening melodies up to a late hour. Flambeaux threw flames into the dark spots, and the archers of the watch united with the king's life guards and castle watch to keep down rough offences.

Guise, after having held a reception which satiated him, sat at his window ledge, soothed by the music of the rippling Loire shooting under the bridge.

Everything seemed to be done to make all visitors retain in pleasant memory this exceptional parliament when peace was promised the distracted kingdom.

The great marplot, and plotter, the old queen, had been induced to stay away. There was even a whisper that Henry of Navarre would be induced to adopt the state religion in good faith and submit to share with Guise the powers not comprised by the king alone.

In fact, there was no rumor, however flighty, which did not receive some heed and some credence.

Guise brooded and became less somber.

The buzz from the town, peopled to five times its regular population, came to his ears. The young nobles, lavish naturally, given the cue by the king's favorites, had turned the palace into a nest of song birds. The songs of the loving, the care-free and the light-hearted pierced even to his secret soul.

He had a vision of a future never before contemplated by him.

He thought that Therine would forget the

sanguinary termination to her brief and silly acquaintance with the Count of St. Megrin, and that, as his duchess, he could pass a few hours at a time with her in as domestic an interior as is permitted to the grandee.

His prospects had, to him, never beamed more dazzlingly.

It was all within the domain of reason that he should defeat Henry of Navarre, the only serious antagonist. Between him and Spain, the best strategists were sure that the hero of the Protestants must be irretrievably crushed. Then, by his union with Clèves, he might be fortified on the throne by German influence.

He had it on his tongue tip to join in the burden of an odd old lay which rovers on the bridge, locking arms, were singing as they merrily swept along, making the proud burghers duck their arms, and opening to let the pretty maids pass—on tax of a kiss.

Their reflections danced on the water.

"I do not think I have ever been so jocund!"

breathed he; and, leaning out of the casement, he sang, too:

> "'I cannot follow you, through stone and mortar!'
> 'Pull down one side, and I, the other!'
> She pulled down the stone and he the timber,
> And their lips met, as we remember!"

At that moment, methodically winding up his huge Nuremberg "egg"—that is, watch—he felt still glad.

He believed that he would harvest by his rashness.

"Fortune's fingers crook on mine," murmured he.

He forbore to call his gentleman to help him disrobe.

He was in his hose and vest when the noise in the streets was hushed; the good folk had not only gone to bed, but their watch had impressed on the wanderers the necessity of retiring also, on the penalty of passing the rest of the night in the watchhouse.

To the music and merry confusion succeeded

the ponderous soundlessness of a massive stone building on high out of the housetop levels.

It was the deep of night.

Except a set prayer inculcated in youth, he rarely uttered one.

But this time he felt that he must not lay his head on his pillow, under which, as usual, was laid his sword, without some call for superior protection.

While he was soliciting the saints, at the outer door of his apartments was acted the following scene—dread, mortal, appalling in its promise:

Vitry did not abate a whit of his faith in St. Megrin killing his foe, but his position in taking up the hateful duty which the brave Crillon repudiated, compelled him to leave not a loophole open in his report to the king.

As the act was personal, imperiling his very soul, he could not allow strangers to enter into his confidence. For subordinates he chose, at the town gates, some disbanded soldiers and the drunken ones expelled for excesses. But for the seconds next to him, he included only his kin; his brother and his brother-in-law, took up posts which effectually cut off communication of Guise's friends with him in his rooms, where he could not "stir or wag" but singly.

Vitry presented himself with the cutthroats, pure and simple, at the first door. St. Megrin kept by his side.

Dumilatre opened to his subdued rap drowsily; he was sleeping in his clothes by a fire in a brazier, as the nights were chill at the river side.

Vitry presented a pistol to his cheek and said in a low, deep voice:

"King's service! Silence, on your life!"

St. Megrin pushed by him during the brief act and was followed in lockstep by the bravoes.

Three gentlemen-in-waiting sprang up, almost as sleepily as their chief. They were too dumfounded by the entrance of desperate armed men to draw their daggers or take down their swords, imprudently hung on the wall pegs.

They were gagged and bound with their own scarfs and laid on the floor. Two or three of the royal guards, without their cassocks and plumed hats, but in morions and blacked steel coats, came in with boots muffled in felt strips, and stood to guard them.

In the apartment, lying on the rug at the inner door, was the trusted valet, by name Griscon, because of that part of Switzerland; as it is known as "the Grey League," the jest went that he was predestined to serve the League in France, too. Be this as it may, he must have been perverted, for, instead of sending up an outcry, as was his bounded duty, and using his halberd, he let himself be secured with the docility of one of the famous cattle of his native mountains.

There was nothing but to go into the bedroom and deal with the master.

Vitry had a fluttering of the heart, and he

glanced searchingly at St. Megrin. The latter was cool as if cut out of a glacier.

Luckily, one of those sudden and short hurrying winds which sweep off the Alps and rush up or down the Loire, arose at this instant. All the weathercocks squeaked as they spun on the pikes; the tower owls and rooks sprang into the air and jostled the frightened pigeons; the great royal standard flapped and spread out, and early-ripened leaves were whirled noisily about the turrets.

In this gust, which quelled any noise their guarded footsteps made, the murderers pushed the door open and dashed in to surround the bed.

But they had to do with a practiced warrior. By instinct rather than any solid foundation for apprehension, Guise had already bounded out of the bed.

He had snatched at his sword as he thus rose. They found him, therefore, not prostrate, but erect, his back against the farther high post of the state couch. His sword, caught up by the blade, was not yet handled properly, for his surprise was extreme, and palsied him.

But the breeze having swept the sky clear of the whirl of dry, falling leaves, rays of starlight flittered in by the small-paned window. He knew Baron Vitry by his office near the king, and still hoped that the communication was not deadly. But, at the second glance, confounding St. Megrin in his mask with the myrmidons, he regained the foreboding which he ought never to have discarded, and he said in a tone of scathing indignation, the more insulting as it expressed his full belief in the king being apt to assassinate:

"You, baron, leading bandits?"

Without heeding this challenge, which showed that his true errand was more than divined, the new captain of guards spoke the traditional words which meant so much to fallen nobles:

"My lord duke, the king commands me to take your sword!"

"The sword with which I have performed so much good service for him!" replied Guise, without giving up the weapon.   In fact, he took his grasp on the hilt to use it, and coolly numbered his foes.

"My lord duke!" said Vitry, continuing his official phrasing, "the king commands me to seize your person!"

This was different. To take a sword was simple imprisonment foretold, and the person might be released from custody. But to have "the body seized," for the king's disposal was giving one up to death—this was not merely the jailer, but the executioner.

But this time, like men who knew their work, the murderers had surrounded the duke literally. Two slipped into the recess between the bed and the wall, and the others formed a half-ring before the prince.

He was so sure that all precautions had been

taken to prevent his escape that he did not raise his voice to summon his men. He cherished not the faintest belief that they had not been made helpless—probably by death, since his person was not sacred.

Bitterly he deplored that he had repelled his brother's advice and the urging of his friends.

"Antraguet not here?" Ah, curses on that beauty whose care had deprived him of his best hand!

Vitry, protected by his sword, stretched out his left hand to clutch the blade which he had claimed as the king's.

It was simply resistance and death, or death without resistance.

Which was most becoming to Henry the Scarface?

He did not waver an instant.

Now, five or six more appeared at the doorway. He was beset.

But a flush of shame spread over him at seeing a Valois do what was so disgraceful in a king of France.

"So you would murder me," said he, scorchingly. "Mark, the murder of the Duke of Guise will go down to posterity as costing as many lives as to kill me on the field of battle! Vitry, degraded knight, craven baron, you and your tools will be returned to the vile master who sent you, broken, broken!"

He fell on guard.

But the last comers had firearms. They advanced, and, laying their gun barrels on the shoulders of their fellows, leveled them at the doomed prince. Besides, the two men in the alcove would pierce him in the back.

Hopeless as was the outlook, still he was about to spring upon the captain.

"Oh, if there had been *one* gentleman here," groaned he, distressed at dying so ignobly and in the dark, "I would have made him a noble; if there had been one honest peasant I would

have made him a knight before my power to do
these things becomes dust and ashes!"

At this Vitry turned pale, and his sword point
was slightly lowered. St. Megrin touched him
on the shoulder and said, slowly:

"It is my turn!"

CHAPTER XIX.

BY THE KING'S COMMAND.

He stepped forward, and the baron receded a little.

The matches were well afire now. They did not blaze, but sent out a dull glow, like dead wood in a burning forest.

Guise saw this lovely figure of the young and graceful man, and perceived that it was not one of the hangers-on at taverns and gaming-houses, ready to slay *for a sovereign* and for a sum.

The mask baffled him, but he thought he recognized an acquaintance.

A poignant moment was this. He went over the whole line of friends whom he had offended and wronged, seeking to particularize one betrayed and who was justified in killing him at midnight; but he was glad that he did not re-

member one toward whom he had been guilty to
this extent.

"You shall not die under the volley; not at
the hired point!" said St. Megrin.   "You are to
die, God deciding, as becomes a knight, though
false, recreant and cruel!"

A blight must have permeated Guise; he
longed to recognize this mellow voice, which
the chastening had perhaps weakened and intense rage made rancid.

"Who are you?   Unmask, if I am to cross
swords with you!"

The king's gallant tore off the mask by breaking the strings.

"St. Megrin!" cried Lorraine, backing so that
the post alone stopped him.

"My lord, you must die now, not to tell that
I came with such attendance," said the other,
haughtily.   "You avoided the chance for a fair
fight by ordering me to be murdered.   Now,
I repay by offering you the fair fight a second
time!   Do you fight or fall butchered?"

The duke responded clearly, if curtly, by sa-
luting his adversary in that form which always
preceded a regular duel.

On seeing this, Vitry made a sign.   His men
retired a little while, keeping their circle and defending the issues.   Those who were ensconced
by the bed leaned on it; it was still under
the guns that the contest was to occur.

Embittered by recalling from it being the
same hour and the surrounding visages twins
to those beleaguering him in Soissons House,
when he had the princess to protect, St. Megrin
could only see that he was now to retaliate,
blow for blow, and that the reward of his victory would be, as in primeval conflicts, the hand
of the woman both sought.

As for the bewildered prince, he felt that this
was a judgment for his having basely let his aris-
tocratic ideas preclude him from punishing his
aggressor with his own hand.   Nevertheless,
if he were to perish, better thus, to his mind,
than by the slaughterers, headed by Vitry, and

made more base because it was by a dastardly monarch's orders.

He was desperate, for, just as he had believed Antraguet would arrange St. Megrin's assassination, he saw no loophole; he must die at the end of all.

The end? In Blois Castle, according to tradition, a deep well and a heavy stone over the dead man lowered into it.

Like a lord accustomed to trappings and embellishments, he further felt stung by his opponent meeting him thus in gloom. If he were to meet death at such hands, he would have chosen the mode King Henry had royally offered—a tourney in a court, surrounded by the dames and knights, the vulgar excluded beyond the palings; heralds, trumpets, banners flying, spears and axes gleaming, much cheering at the dextrous defense and at the gallant attacks.

This count, in travel-worn habits, with a war sword replacing the one Schomberg had left uselessly to his avenger, his resentful mien, his determined carriage, all the looks of a bloodthirsty fighter. Altogether like "the Rough Tilter" who, covered with armor to the crown of his head, entered the lists one day before King Louis XI., and, without a name, defeated every jouster to the highest. Then, carrying the crown of victory on his lance tip contemptuously, he had ridden away, still unnamed, and the legend said it was Death in person!

St. Megrin was his *Angst-mann*, as they said in his country, more than his executioner, his expiationist, who gave anguish with the last stroke.

So he entered on the struggle with misgivings nigh to despair, expecting no possible satisfaction but to inflict death to this one, at least.

The action between men of the same degree of skill and strength and courage could not be lasting. Indeed, its duration might have been limited by Vitry's impatience; he felt that he would be blamed for this unaccountable pro-crastination. Macbeth understood these state assassinations, when he said: "If it were done when 'tis done, then 'twere well it were done quickly."

From the first clash of the steel, both com-prehended that the duke had been wise to meet his enemy by proxies. All the experience of warfare could not compensate for that youth which would "serve." Then, the younger man was deeply assured if only by his angel's last glance, full of gratitude, love and promise, that he would, if he joined hand to hand with hers at the altar, go through life led thus by her.

Three lunges had been interchanged and two cuts, and then both, after a feint, thrust tre-mendously at the same time. It became not a test of skill or power, but of the worth of the metal. The point of Guise's weapon, blunted by having ground on the steel tip of the scab-bard, was fixed, as if a chisel driven by a mal-let, in the interstices of St. Megrin's Spanish guard—a round plate; it bent, and, had it been of more brittle metal, would have snapped, and with the truncheon he might rapidly have hewn down his antagonist, carried by him by the force of the advance. On the other hand, warded off a little, St. Megrin's point entered the folds of his shirt, raised up at the waist belt by the struggle, and there entangled, bent double and flew out, after slightly wounding him under the heart. In this thrust, the nipped blade followed his. Guise would not let go, but his wrist was terribly wrenched. St. Megrin, like the other, had his dagger out, used more for parrying a missed blow than to stab, but it was authorized, at this period in the duello, to employ it in any manner.

He raised his left hand and brought it down with all his force upon the neck, inside the collar-bone of the prince. The blow alone would have felled an ox. The duke staggered.

Both swords fell to the floor.

But the staggering one was lost. The blade

had gone down into the lungs, for on the lips, convulsed with pain and baffled passion, bloody froth immediately appeared, with an execration, had it been half-fulfilled, all present would have been overwhelmed by the castle in ruins.

"Ah, crooked fortune!" gasped the duke.

The sight of the dying one, as he tottered and threw up his arms, the groan, the peculiar fury which seizes men used to bloodshed and spurring them, incited all to fall on and "leave his notch" on the tree.

All who had firearms let fly the shot, at the risk of hitting a friend; the rest rushed onto the now prostrate body like wolves on a stricken buck.

St. Megrin was hurled aside.

But his passing pity was curbed by his assurance that he had, betimes, been the death of Therine's persecutor.

That hand, crisping up in lockjaw, would never again crush her arm; that tyrant would not crush her heart, with its growing love!

" The rest rushed on the now prostrate body, like wolves on a stricken
buck."   See page 296.

None the less, he was about to enter into the horrible medley when he refrained at the hiss, like a serpent's, at the door.

Holding back the hangings with a white and slender hand, a man thrust in his head. That he was allowed to penetrate to where the murder was perpetrated, proclaimed him to be uniquely privileged.

"The king!" came warningly from behind this apparition.

Vitry looked around. Over the pale but joyous, and yet anxious, countenance of Valois, were those of his brother, Hallier, and his brother-in-law.

He made a sign that all was over, for the benefit of the three.

Then Henry stepped into the room with the shuddering and trepidation of one barefoot, who fears to plash into blood.

The slayers moved aside, and bowed as they smiled, knowing who had been the true employer. They were jealous that St. Megrin should not reap all the advantages which they perceived would fall in showers.

"Good! I am king—I am free of my nightmare!" said he, in a stronger voice. "You are captain, Vitry!"

Then, bending over the dead body, stretched on its back by the last spasm, he added, without looking up:

"Who got in the first blow?"

Vitry had already received his reward; he generously unscreened St. Megrin, and said:

"He is here, my lord!"

Some one had lighted a torch in the outer rooms; it was brought into the dorway. Henry recognized his favorite.

He had thought him dead of his wounds. It was next to the same surprise, in degree, which he would have felt had Guise revived.

"Paul Stuart? St. Megrin?"

"Did I not promise your majesty that I would not spare him if we met hand to hand?" said the gallant, proudly.

"Yes, yes; but you bleed!"

"Your grace, love must stanch the blood shed in this duel!"

"Hem!" coughed the king, drawing away his eyes, still fascinated, from his enemy, his rival, his balked successor. "I think I guess—you are enamored with his lady?"

The murderers had withdrawn so far from the two that Henry felt the awe of being alone with the dead. He took St. Megrin by the arm and led him toward the door.

"He was alone! he had not his brother with him——"

"Mayenne?"

"Yes! the other has danced with him!"

The king had inscribed the Cardinal of Lorraine's name beside his brother's on the death roll! Slay a prince of the church? How vindictive was this weakling when deeply moved! The cardinal was also slain.

But the king should not linger here. The

shots had aroused not only all in the place, but many in the town.

A few of Guise's adherents in the castle talked of rescue and then of vengeance. But at the words uttered by officials, right and left: "The king's will is done!" all objection ceased. But no one laid down to sleep that morning.

As for Mayenne, he had fled to his governorship of Burgundy, where he raised all his forces to avenge the double homicide.

In vain did the upholders of Valois maintain that it was a private duel in which the Prince of Lorraine fell; history ignores the chronicle and calls it assassination. The blood spot is still shown in the castle.

When Jacques Clement murdered Henry III. to the applause of the Parisians, whose idol the Great Guise had been, in summer, 1589, people called it the answering stroke of heavenly judgment.

That timely poet, the street songmaker, went down into the crossings and recited:

"Worst of the Valois' useless strain,
  Broken in health, mind, reign and word,
By a pig-sticker's knife was slain,
  Because not worthy of the hangman's sword!"

St. Megrin, like Crillon, went over to his legitimate successor, Henry IV., and accompanied both in their glorious actions.

At the victory of Coutras, he saw the two brothers Joyeuse slain in a heroic charge. And, after the action, when the vanquishers feasted in the great hall of Coutras Castle and the dead lay in the vaults, mocked by the drunken soldiers, he heard with a warming heart, King Henry say:

"This is the time for tears—some for the brave vanquished!"

Epernon went over to the Protestant chief, when he recanted, and was in the coach when he was assassinated by Ravaillac. Accused of having acquiesced in this tragedy, he lived long to repent—if guilty.

The aging queen-mother, having lost three sons—kings—by death, and a fourth who just missed the crown by a mysterious fate, "not wholly free from suspicion of poison," says the recorder, passed away during the religious strife, on the same scene as witnessed Guise's death—in Blois Castle—utterly unlamented, in 1589.

Ruggieri? He passed away as became a genuine magician. During the Paris siege, King Henry IV.'s light horse charged into the town and upon Soissons House, where, foiled in their attempt to capture the poisoner of Queen Joan of Navarre, they set fire to his laboratory. Shrieks were heard in the flames; some said that they came from "his bottled spirits"; others from the wizard, caught in a hiding-place. But the wiseacres asserted, when his dreaded name was mentioned, that he had slipped away, and, with his tainted funds, bought a nook in his own country, where he posed as a patriarch amid a bevy of grandchildren; it was they who, profiting by his recipes, gained a great renown as pyrotechnists.

Disgusted with politics, of which the knots were cut by the knife, St. Megrin, whose dukedom had been confirmed by the fourth Henry, was so appalled by twice losing his royal masters by the same death, that he retired with his duchess to her own paternal estates on the Rhine. But, unfortunately, at the death of her father the whole of that region was rent by war, religious, local and imperial, and he departed into Italy, where he passed his declining years with his wife, sympathetic in the pursuit of letters and collecting paintings and ancient art.

The fate of Bussy the Brave, is detailed in the "Lady of Monsoreau."

So passed the last and the best of the king's gallants.

THE END.